The Lost King's Crown

Freya Jobe

Published by Freya Jobe, 2024.

This is a work of fiction. Similarities to real people, places, or events are entirely coincidental.

THE LOST KING'S CROWN

First edition. November 4, 2024.

Copyright © 2024 Freya Jobe.

ISBN: 979-8224721108

Written by Freya Jobe.

The Lost King's Crown
A young squire must find the lost crown before dawn to save the kingdom.

The kingdom of Eldoria lay cloaked in silence, an unsettling stillness that no one dared disturb. The castle's towers, usually ablaze with torchlight, were darkened under the heavy blanket of night, and the people waited in hushed fear. It was the eve of the Celestial Dawn—a sacred day foretold by ancient prophets to bring either unmatched prosperity or ruin, depending on the fate of the king's crown.

For generations, the crown of Eldoria had been more than just a symbol of the king's rule. Forged by the first mage-king centuries ago, it was imbued with powerful magic meant to protect the realm. Rumours whispered that it held a piece of Eldoria's very soul, guarding the land from war, famine, and the dark curses of neighbouring kingdoms. But the crown was not only a blessing. Bound by a terrible prophecy, it was said that should the crown be lost or defiled, Eldoria would fall into an age of darkness from which it would never recover.

Tonight, the unthinkable had happened. Just as the Celestial Dawn's moon rose high above the kingdom, an ominous cry rang through the castle halls—the crown had been stolen. Guards searched the castle in vain, and the king, weakened by an inexplicable illness, lay barely clinging to life. Panic spread as those who knew the legend understood that without the crown, Eldoria would soon crumble.

In the shadows of the great hall, a young squire named Finn watched the chaos unfold. Small for his age but filled with quiet determination, he had served in the castle for as long as he could remember, honing his skills and dreaming of someday becoming a knight. But as he witnessed the fear in the eyes of those around him, Finn felt an unfamiliar tug in his chest. He knew little of magic or prophecy, but something within him stirred—a sense of duty, of purpose, ignited.

With his heart pounding, Finn approached the throne room, where he overheard the gravest of conversations. He learned that the curse would fall at dawn if the crown was not returned, and that there was no one left who could—or would—seek it out. The king, fighting through his fever, gave a single command, weak but resolute: "Find the crown. Save our kingdom."

The squire had little time to ponder the risks. Gathering his courage, he slipped away from the bustling guards and made his way toward the castle gates. The crown must be retrieved before dawn, and no one else would—or could—rise to the challenge. For a young squire, untrained and unknown, this was a calling greater than any knighthood. The fate of Eldoria now rested on his shoulders.

Thus, as the kingdom held its breath, Finn embarked on a journey into the night, one that would lead him through enchanted forests, past dangerous foes, and deep into the mysteries of the lost crown. It was a journey that would not only determine the future of Eldoria but also shape the boy who would come to be known as its bravest hero.

Act 1: The Call to Adventure

Chapter 1: The Kingdom's Dark Hour

The kingdom of Eldoria lay silent under the cloak of midnight, each shadow stretched thin beneath the full moon's cold, silver gaze. Stars glittered in a clear sky, a rare sight above the castle, as if even the heavens held their breath, waiting. The wind barely stirred the banners that hung over the castle walls, each bearing the sigil of the king—a golden crown encircled by a ring of stars, symbolizing protection and unity. Yet tonight, an eerie stillness had taken over the land.

Within the castle walls, Finn, a young squire no older than sixteen, lay sound asleep in the small servants' quarters. He shared the cramped room with three other squires, their cots lined up like soldiers at attention. Finn's breathing was steady, deep, his face softened in rest. His days were long and full of tasks, with duties that required him to move swiftly and quietly through the castle halls, polishing armour, gathering supplies, running messages for knights or cooks alike. And though he worked hard, he rarely felt tired; tonight, however, his dreams were heavy and strange, as if shadows had seeped into his sleep, whispering things just beyond his understanding.

Unbeknownst to Finn and the rest of the castle's inhabitants, something terrible had occurred just before midnight. The king's crown—the symbol of his rule, of Eldoria's strength and magic—was gone.

The theft had been discovered by an elderly guard making his usual rounds. Old Bryndel had been one of the king's trusted sentries for decades, his watchful eyes missing nothing. Yet tonight, as he turned the corner into the Royal Treasury, he found the chamber empty, its guards slumped over in a deep, unnatural sleep. Panic surged through him, and he knew, even before his eyes confirmed it, that the crown was gone.

A sharp, sick feeling twisted his stomach as he took in the scene. The heavy wooden door of the treasury had been cracked open, and the gold pedestal where the crown rested stood bare. This crown was no ordinary object; it was said to hold the protective magic of Eldoria itself. Bryndel's trembling hand rose to his forehead, a silent prayer escaping his lips. He knew the ancient prophecy by heart, as every guard did. It foretold that if the crown were ever lost, Eldoria would fall to ruin with the coming dawn.

Word spread through the castle like wildfire, reaching the highest officials first, then trickling down to the knights and trusted servants. Whispers of the theft and the prophecy passed quickly from person to person, each version more dreadful than the last. The castle's tension grew, palpable, a creeping dread that slipped through the stone halls and up into the chambers of the royal family.

But here, in the servants' quarters, there was only the soft sound of Finn's breathing, the quiet creak of his cot as he turned, oblivious to the storm brewing outside his door. He was lost in a deep sleep, his dreams untouched by the turmoil.

As the minutes wore on, more and more people were roused from their beds to join the search. The guards hurried from chamber to chamber, gathering information, scouring every corner of the castle for any sign of the thief. Some of the knights, armed and ready, had taken to the stables, preparing their horses in case they needed to search beyond the castle grounds. The high priests of the temple had been summoned, their faces pale and drawn as they gathered to perform ancient rites, prayers slipping from their lips as they pleaded for protection against whatever darkness had dared breach their walls.

But the crown was nowhere to be found.

In the throne room, the king lay slumped in his grand chair, his eyes glazed with exhaustion. Though he'd been roused from bed the moment the theft was discovered, he seemed unable to fully awaken, his words slurred and weak. His chief advisor, Lord Aldric, stood nearby, casting worried glances at the ailing king. It was as if the very absence of the crown had cast a pall over him, draining him of strength, leaving him vulnerable.

"Where is it, Aldric?" the king murmured, his voice barely a whisper. "How could this happen?"

Aldric placed a hand on his shoulder. "We will find it, Your Majesty. Our best men are on the search, and they will not rest until the crown is returned."

The king tried to sit up, his hand clutching his chest as if something unseen weighed upon him. "The prophecy... it cannot be true. Not now... not my kingdom."

But Aldric's own heart was heavy. He knew the prophecy as well as any in Eldoria, perhaps even better. It had been a tale of legends, a cautionary tale told to frighten young children. Yet tonight, with the crown missing and the king visibly weakening, Aldric feared it was no mere story.

Hours dragged by, each passing minute inching closer to dawn. Servants, knights, and guards continued to comb through the castle and grounds, every corner, every passage, even the secret rooms only a few knew of. Yet no sign of the crown or the thief appeared. It was as though the earth itself had swallowed it.

In the midst of this chaos, Finn's sleep grew troubled. His brow furrowed, his breaths quickened. He saw flashes of darkness in his dreams—a winding path through a forest, shadows flickering in the corners of his vision, strange voices whispering words he couldn't quite make out. His hands felt heavy in his dream, like they were clutching something precious and fragile, but he couldn't see what it was.

Suddenly, a loud noise jolted him awake. His eyes flew open, his heart pounding as he tried to orient himself in the dim, moonlit room. The others stirred slightly in their cots but remained asleep, undisturbed. He held his breath, listening intently. Footsteps echoed down the hallway outside, hurried and urgent.

Slowly, he sat up, still half-lost in the dream's fog. A strange sense of urgency lingered within him, as though his body remembered something he couldn't grasp. Blinking away the sleep, he ran a hand through his tousled hair, glancing toward the door. He considered lying back down, but something in his gut wouldn't let him. It felt... wrong, as though a weight pressed upon him, urging him to move, to act.

After a moment's hesitation, he swung his legs over the side of the cot and slipped his boots on, his movements careful and quiet so as not to wake the others. He crept toward the door, opened it just enough to peer out. The hallway was dimly lit by the moon filtering in through the narrow windows, casting long shadows along the stone floor. But he could hear voices, low and tense, coming from further down.

Curiosity piqued, he stepped out into the corridor. He recognized one of the voices as belonging to Bryndel, the elderly guard. Bryndel's tone was clipped, anxious—a sound Finn wasn't used to hearing from the normally unflappable guard.

"...the king is growing weaker," Bryndel said, his voice hushed but clear. "They say he may not last until dawn without the crown."

A lump formed in Finn's throat as he processed the words. The crown? The king's crown, the one kept in the Royal Treasury, was missing? He hadn't heard anything about it, but then again, he was just a squire. He rarely caught wind of important news until long after everyone else.

Still, an inexplicable dread settled in his stomach as he edged closer to listen.

"If we can't find it..." another voice began, but the words faded, leaving Finn to fill in the blanks. Find what? What had happened to the king?

Bryndel and the other guard moved off down the hall, their footsteps fading into silence, leaving Finn alone in the cold corridor. He clenched his hands, feeling his pulse quicken. Something was terribly wrong. And though he didn't know why, he felt as if he were somehow connected to it all, as though a hidden hand were guiding him.

Turning back to the empty room behind him, Finn made a decision. Whatever was happening in the castle tonight, he was going to find out.

He took a deep breath, steeling himself, and stepped quietly down the corridor, his heart pounding with a strange, new determination.

Chapter 2: The Unlikely Hero

Finn awoke the next morning, not to the soft glow of dawn creeping over the castle, but to the loud clamour of hurried footsteps and frantic whispers outside his quarters. He rubbed his eyes, disoriented, trying to piece together the muffled sounds from beyond the thick stone walls. The urgency in the voices was unmistakable. Servants were rushing through the halls, their murmurs blending into an incoherent hum of worry and confusion.

Curiosity sparked, Finn swung his legs out of bed and dressed quickly, his heart racing as he imagined the possible reasons for the commotion. The castle rarely stirred this early unless there was a special event or a crisis. Today was supposed to be ordinary, a quiet day of training, chores, and maybe a few stolen moments in the courtyard to practice his swordplay. Yet, from the sounds in the hallway, it was clear that something extraordinary—or disastrous—had happened.

Stepping out of his small chamber, he glanced around, trying to catch snippets of conversation from passing servants. But all he got were hurried nods, anxious expressions, and vague responses when he asked what was happening. He spotted a fellow squire, Garon, leaning against the wall, pale and wide-eyed.

"Garon!" Finn called, moving toward him. "What's going on?"

Garon shook his head, looking dazed. "I'm not sure, but it's bad, Finn. Real bad. They're saying something... something's missing. Something important."

"Missing?" Finn echoed, frowning. "What could be so important that it would cause all this fuss?"

But Garon just shrugged, casting a nervous glance down the corridor. "I don't know. They're telling everyone to stay in their quarters. They're looking for someone to blame, I think."

Finn's curiosity only grew. A missing item? People to blame? His mind raced through a list of objects that might be valuable enough to cause an uproar, but nothing seemed to fit. A chill crept up his spine as he thought of the treasures held within the castle walls. Whatever it was, it must be something deeply connected to the king himself.

Determined to find out more, Finn slipped away from Garon and made his way toward the main hall, where he hoped to catch a clearer word on what was happening. He took the back staircases, avoiding the crowded corridors, and emerged near the great hall, hidden behind one of the tall stone pillars that lined the room. From there, he could see a gathering of nobles, guards, and advisors, all engaged in intense discussion. At the head of the group stood Sir Alric, the captain of the guard, his brow furrowed in anger.

Finn strained to hear but couldn't catch their words. Still, their expressions told him enough—whatever had happened was serious, far more serious than he'd imagined. Sir Alric barked orders, and a group of guards hurried out of the hall, their footsteps echoing as they disappeared down the corridor.

The sight of Sir Alric's grim face sent a shiver down Finn's spine. He had heard the stories about the captain of the guard, a man who had served the kingdom loyally for decades. Sir Alric was known for his unwavering dedication to the king and his fierce, unyielding sense of justice. If he was this disturbed, it meant that something truly important had been lost, something that could threaten the stability of the entire kingdom.

Finn took a step back, trying to process what he'd seen, but his foot slipped on the smooth stone floor, making a faint sound that seemed to echo through the empty hall. He froze, holding his breath, but Sir Alric's keen eyes had already spotted him.

"Squire!" Sir Alric's voice rang out, sharp and commanding. "What are you doing here?"

Finn's heart raced, but he forced himself to stand tall as he stepped out from behind the pillar. "My apologies, Sir Alric," he stammered. "I— I heard the commotion. I didn't mean to intrude."

Sir Alric studied him, his gaze piercing, as though he could see right through Finn's nervous facade. "What did you hear?"

"Nothing, sir," Finn replied quickly, his voice steady. "I only saw the crowd and wanted to know if there was anything I could do to help."

The captain's eyes narrowed, but after a moment, he gave a brisk nod. "Return to your quarters, squire. This is not a matter for you or any of the castle's youth. Let those who are trained and trusted handle it."

Finn nodded, backing away slowly, his mind still racing. As he turned to leave, he couldn't help but notice the troubled expressions on the faces of the gathered nobles. There was a fear in their eyes, an apprehension that seemed to cloud the air around them. Whatever they were dealing with, it was no ordinary theft or loss.

As he walked back toward his quarters, Finn's thoughts churned. He felt certain that this was something more, something that would have far-reaching consequences beyond what any of the nobles were willing to admit aloud. He couldn't shake the feeling that this was no mere accident—that whatever had happened, it was the work of someone with a plan, someone who understood the secrets of the castle far too well.

Back in his quarters, he paced, replaying everything he'd seen and heard. His instincts told him that there was a plot unfolding, a conspiracy that reached higher than anyone might suspect. And even though Sir Alric had dismissed him, Finn felt a gnawing need to learn more, to understand the full extent of what was at stake. After all, this was his home, too. The kingdom he had served, even as a lowly squire, meant everything to him.

Little did he know that he was already entangled in the very heart of the mystery, bound by fate to a mission that would soon test every ounce of his courage. For Finn was no ordinary squire, and though he had no way of knowing it, he would soon become the unlikely hero Eldoria needed.

Chapter 3: A Dangerous Secret

Finn couldn't sleep. The unsettling events of the morning lingered in his mind, leaving him restless and alert. Shadows seemed to stretch further in his quarters, and the hushed murmurs that drifted through the hallways were laced with fear. He felt a heavy weight pressing down on him, an inexplicable urge to know more, to understand what was truly happening within the castle walls.

When the castle grew quiet again, he decided to sneak out. Something important had been lost, and it was clear that the castle guards were frantic to retrieve it. But what could possibly hold enough power to throw everyone into such a state of disarray? He thought about the rumours he'd heard over the years—the legendary treasures, the ancient relics rumoured to protect Eldoria. But those had always seemed like tales for the firelight, stories to inspire young squires like him to dream of glory.

Keeping to the shadows, Finn crept through the dimly lit corridors, his heart pounding in his chest. The guards had increased their patrols, and every corner was more heavily watched than usual, making it difficult to remain unseen. But his years of tending to chores and running errands had taught him every hidden pathway and narrow stairwell in the castle. He knew exactly where to go to avoid detection.

As he approached the main hall, he noticed light spilling out from the door of a small side chamber. Voices echoed softly from within, and he immediately recognized the deep, commanding tone of Sir Alric. Finn slipped behind a tapestry and leaned closer, straining to catch the words.

"We have until dawn," Sir Alric said, his voice heavy with urgency. "If we don't retrieve the crown by then... the curse will fall upon us all."

Finn froze, his mind racing. The crown? He had heard legends about it, of course—the symbol of the king's authority, an ancient artifact said to contain powerful magic. But he had never understood its significance. Now, hearing Sir Alric speak with such intensity, he realized the crown was far more than just a royal adornment.

A curse, bound to the crown. And they had only until dawn to recover it.

The other voice, softer but equally tense, belonged to Lady Eveline, the king's chief advisor. "We should inform the people," she urged. "They deserve to know the danger we face. This is not just a matter of royal pride; it's about the survival of Eldoria itself."

"No," Sir Alric replied sharply. "Panic will spread like wildfire. We must keep this secret. The kingdom's stability depends on it. Only the most trusted guards and advisors know, and it must stay that way."

"But what about the prophecy?" Lady Eveline pressed. "It foretold that should the crown be lost on the eve of the Celestial Dawn, a darkness would sweep over Eldoria, plunging us into ruin."

"We will find it," Sir Alric said with iron determination. "We must."

Finn's heart thundered in his chest. The prophecy, the Celestial Dawn, the curse—all of it came crashing down on him like a tidal wave. He had heard whispers of the prophecy in passing, a tale told by the older squires to frighten each other on cold, dark nights. But he had never believed it to be anything more than a myth. Yet here it was, real and terrifying.

The crown had been stolen, and if it wasn't returned by dawn, the kingdom would face devastation.

As Sir Alric and Lady Eveline continued their conversation in lower voices, Finn barely dared to breathe. The implications of what he had overheard settled heavily on his shoulders. Eldoria was on the brink of ruin, and no one outside this small circle of trusted advisors even knew the truth. The kingdom's safety depended on their ability to find the crown, and time was slipping away.

A part of him wanted to run, to retreat to his quarters and try to forget the dangerous knowledge he'd just stumbled upon. But he couldn't. He was a squire, trained to serve and protect the kingdom, and while he wasn't yet a knight, he knew he couldn't stand idly by while everything he cared about was at stake. His stomach churned as he realized the full weight of his responsibility.

Suddenly, he heard footsteps approaching from the hall. He held his breath and pressed himself deeper into the shadows, watching as a group of guards entered the chamber. Sir Alric and Lady Eveline's voices fell silent, replaced by the sound of hurried discussions and orders being given.

The guards were briefed quickly and then sent out in groups, each given a different area of the kingdom to search. The urgency in their movements was unmistakable; they had all been told about the curse and the consequences of failure.

Once the room emptied, Finn let out a shaky breath, waiting until the last echoes of footsteps faded before daring to move. His mind spun with questions. Who had stolen the crown? Why now, on the eve of such a critical moment? And how could he, a young squire with no training in magic or prophecy, do anything to help?

But even as doubts clouded his thoughts, a tiny flicker of determination grew within him. He knew the castle, its passageways, its hidden rooms. And he had overheard enough to understand what was at stake. If the advisors and knights couldn't recover the crown in time, maybe he could help—if only by searching the places they'd overlooked or running messages between the search parties. Whatever he could do, he was ready to try.

As he slipped away from the chamber, he felt the weight of the dangerous secret settle over him like a cloak. No one else knew the true threat facing Eldoria, and he couldn't share it—not with the other squires, not with his friends, not even with the kind kitchen maid who had often treated him to extra helpings of soup. This burden was his alone.

Finn knew he had to be careful. Every minute counted, and with dawn drawing closer, he felt the ticking clock in every beat of his heart.

The kingdom's future hung by a thread, and he was now part of a mission far larger than himself.

Chapter 4: The King's Last Command

Finn's footsteps echoed faintly as he crept through the winding corridors of the castle, his mind still racing with the chilling secret he had overheard. Somewhere in these walls, the crown had been hidden or whisked away, and with it, the kingdom's fate lay in peril. He kept to the shadows, avoiding the roving guards and the anxious servants who scurried about with hushed urgency. The entire castle felt like it was holding its breath, waiting for something dark and inevitable to descend.

As he passed a corridor leading to the royal chambers, he noticed an unusual number of guards stationed outside the king's door. Some of them were whispering, their faces lined with worry, while others stood silent, gripping their spears with white-knuckled tension. Finn hesitated, the sight sparking his curiosity. Why were so many guards positioned here? The king had been ill for weeks, but never had his chambers been so heavily guarded.

Before he could think better of it, he found himself approaching the guards. He was only a squire, but something about the energy in the air felt urgent, and he sensed that this was exactly where he needed to be.

One of the guards, noticing his approach, narrowed his eyes. "What are you doing here, squire?"

Finn straightened, hoping to mask his nerves with a show of confidence. "I came to see if there's anything I can do to help, sir."

The guard hesitated, glancing back toward the door. "The king... he's been asking for someone. He's weak, barely coherent. But he keeps insisting."

"Insisting on what?" Finn asked, his curiosity deepening.

The guard sighed. "He's been calling for a squire. We assumed he meant Sir Alric's youngest, but... Alric thinks he might mean someone else." He looked Finn up and down, as if sizing him up. "Perhaps it's you he's been calling."

Finn's heart pounded. The king, asking for a squire? And of all the squires, could he truly mean Finn? The guard's expression softened, as though he recognized the confusion and fear flickering in Finn's eyes. Finally, he stepped aside, gesturing for Finn to enter.

Inside, the royal chamber was dimly lit, with heavy curtains drawn over the windows. The air was thick with the scent of medicinal herbs and incense. By the side of the grand bed, a healer was murmuring softly, her hands hovering over the king, who lay propped up on a stack of pillows. His face was pale, his breathing shallow, and his eyes were half-closed, a distant look clouding his gaze.

Finn swallowed, feeling a strange mixture of awe and dread as he approached the king's bedside. He had never been this close to the ruler of Eldoria, the man who had guided the kingdom with wisdom and strength for as long as he could remember. Now, this powerful figure looked frail, his skin ashen, his form shrunken beneath the thick blankets.

The healer looked up as Finn approached and nodded silently, stepping back to give him space.

As Finn knelt by the king's side, the monarch's eyes shifted toward him, faint recognition sparking within them. The king reached out a trembling hand, his fingers brushing weakly against Finn's shoulder. Finn leaned closer, his heart thudding in his chest.

"Your Majesty," Finn whispered, struggling to find words. "I am here."

The king's voice was barely more than a whisper, his words faint but laced with urgency. "The crown..." he rasped, his voice cracking. "The crown... it must be found."

Finn swallowed, nodding. "Yes, Your Majesty. They're searching for it. Sir Alric and the others... they'll find it."

But the king shook his head slowly, a look of frustration in his eyes. "No... they... they don't understand." His breath came in shallow gasps, his eyes glassy with pain. "The prophecy... the Celestial Dawn. It's... all coming true."

Finn listened, feeling the weight of the king's words settle over him like a heavy cloak. The king's expression was one of desperation, a look Finn had never imagined seeing on such a powerful figure.

"Listen to me, boy," the king whispered, his grip tightening with surprising strength. "They cannot know. Only one who is untainted by greed... unspoiled by ambition... can recover the crown."

The words left Finn feeling as if the room had shrunk around him. "But, Your Majesty," he stammered, "I... I don't know where to begin."

The king's gaze grew more intense, as though he were peering into Finn's very soul. "You have a pure heart, Finn. One not weighed down by pride or politics. I have seen it." He took a shuddering breath, pausing to steady himself. "Find the witch, the one they call the Keeper of Shadows. She will guide you... if she believes you are worthy."

Finn felt a chill run down his spine. The Keeper of Shadows was a figure of legend, a reclusive witch who lived beyond the kingdom's borders. Few dared to speak her name, and even fewer had ever seen her. She was rumoured to know the secrets of the old magic, a magic that ran deeper than the rivers and forests of Eldoria itself.

"But how will I find her?" Finn asked, his voice barely a whisper.

The king closed his eyes, his breathing shallow. For a moment, Finn feared he had already slipped away. But then the king's voice came again, weaker this time, like a fading echo. "Follow the river... until it bends under the shadow of the ancient oak. She will find you... if you're meant to be found."

The king's hand fell away, his strength depleted. He slumped back against the pillows, his eyes fluttering closed. The healer rushed forward, her hands hovering over his chest, murmuring softly in an attempt to soothe his pain. Finn backed away, a sense of awe and terror mingling in his heart. The king had given him a mission—a command that could determine the fate of the kingdom itself.

He turned to leave, but the healer stopped him, her gaze fierce. "Whatever he told you, squire, heed it well. The king's words may be faint, but they hold the weight of destiny."

Finn nodded, the weight of the responsibility settling on him like a tangible force. He left the chamber, his mind reeling with the enormity of what had just happened. He was just a squire, barely old enough to wield a sword with confidence. Yet here he was, entrusted by the king himself with the most crucial mission Eldoria had ever known.

As he made his way through the empty halls, Finn's steps grew more purposeful, his heart steadying with newfound resolve. He didn't know what awaited him beyond the kingdom's borders or how he would find the Keeper of Shadows, but he knew he had to try. The king had believed in him, had seen something in him that no one else had.

The crown had to be found before dawn, or all would be lost. Eldoria's fate rested on his shoulders now, and there was no turning back.

With the king's last command ringing in his ears, Finn set off into the night, ready to face whatever dangers lay ahead. The journey would be long, the path unknown, but he was no longer just a squire. He was now the kingdom's only hope.

Chapter 5: The Witch's Warning

The forest seemed to grow darker with each step Finn took, as if it sensed his arrival and closed in around him, watching him with unseen eyes. He shivered, pulling his cloak tighter as he followed the river that twisted and turned beneath the trees. Just as the king had said, he continued until he reached the spot where the river bent under the shadow of an ancient oak, its massive branches stretching out like skeletal fingers against the night sky.

Finn glanced around, uncertain. He half expected the witch to appear from the shadows, but the clearing was silent, save for the gentle burbling of the river and the rustle of leaves in the wind. He hesitated, wondering if he had misunderstood the king's instructions.

Just as he was about to turn back, a soft voice floated through the trees, low and lilting like a melody from another world.

"Why does a squire come seeking secrets in the darkest hour of night?"

Finn whirled around, his heart racing. Standing before him, as if she had materialized from the air itself, was an old woman cloaked in dark, tattered robes. Her hair was wild, cascading over her shoulders in silver waves, and her eyes glimmered with a strange light. She regarded him with a mixture of curiosity and amusement, a faint smile playing on her lips.

Swallowing his fear, Finn mustered the courage to speak. "I... I was sent by the king. He told me that you might be able to help me find the crown."

The witch's smile faded, and a shadow passed over her face. "The crown," she repeated softly, almost to herself. Her gaze drifted past him, as if she were looking at something only she could see. "Yes, I felt its absence. A piece of the kingdom's spirit torn away. Without it, darkness will soon find its way to every corner of Eldoria."

THE LOST KING'S CROWN

Finn took a hesitant step closer. "Please, I need to find it before dawn. The king said... he said you would guide me, if I'm worthy."

The witch's piercing gaze returned to him, her eyes narrowing as she studied him intently. She was silent for a long moment, as though weighing something within him. Finally, she spoke, her voice barely more than a whisper. "Worthiness is a fragile thing, squire. It shifts like the winds and can change with a single choice. But you have come this far, and perhaps that is enough."

She took a step closer, her presence filling the small clearing with an energy that seemed to hum in the air. "Listen well, Finn of Eldoria," she murmured. "I will give you a prophecy, but heed my words carefully, for they are bound in riddles and shadows. The path before you is treacherous, and only a heart unclouded by fear may find the way."

Finn nodded, his heart pounding. He leaned forward, hanging on her every word.

The witch closed her eyes, her voice deepening as she began to chant, a strange rhythm forming in her words:

"In shadows cast by silver light,
A crown lies hidden from all sight.
Beyond the river, past the thorn,
Where truths are buried, and lies are born.
Three trials guard the ancient prize,
Each crafted to reveal disguise.
First is courage, bold and true,
To face what hides inside of you.
Second, wisdom, keen and bright,
To see through dark and find the light.
Third, a heart of purest grace,
To stand for others in their place.
Only one who passes all,
Shall hear the lost king's silent call."

The words seemed to echo around him, lingering in the air like mist. Finn shivered, trying to absorb the meaning hidden within her prophecy. Three trials—courage, wisdom, and grace. But where? How would he even begin to find them?

The witch's eyes opened, and her gaze softened as she looked at him. "These trials will not come to you in obvious ways, young squire. They lie in the choices you make, the fears you face, and the people you encounter. Some will test your body, others your mind, and a few will test the very core of who you are."

Finn felt a tremor of doubt creeping into his heart. "What if... what if I fail?"

The witch placed a gentle, gnarled hand on his shoulder, her voice steady but grave. "Then the darkness will claim you, as it will claim this kingdom. The curse will fall upon Eldoria, and everything you hold dear will be swallowed by shadow."

The enormity of his task settled over him, the weight of it almost too much to bear. But beneath his fear, a flicker of determination remained. He had come this far, and he could not turn back now. Not when the lives of everyone he cared about hung in the balance.

"Is there anything else you can tell me?" he asked, his voice barely more than a whisper.

The witch nodded slowly, her expression thoughtful. "Remember this: not all who seem enemies are foes, and not all allies are what they seem. The path will twist and turn, and the trials will test you in ways you do not expect. Trust in yourself, Finn, and in the strength that lies within you, even if others cannot see it."

Finn clenched his fists, her words burning into his memory. He was just a squire, young and inexperienced, but he knew he had to try. For his kingdom, for his king, and for himself.

The witch released her grip on his shoulder, stepping back into the shadows. "Now go," she said, her voice fading like a distant echo. "The night wanes, and dawn waits for no one. Time is against you, Finn of Eldoria."

Before he could respond, she was gone, her form dissolving into the darkness as though she had never been there. Only the faint whisper of her prophecy lingered in the clearing, wrapping around him like a thread of fate.

Finn took a deep breath, steadying himself as he turned back toward the castle. Three trials awaited him—tests of courage, wisdom, and grace—and he had no idea where or how they would present themselves. All he knew was that he could not afford to fail.

With the witch's warning heavy on his heart, Finn set off into the night, ready to face whatever awaited him. For if he succeeded, he would recover the crown and save Eldoria. But if he failed, he would doom them all.

Chapter 6: Gathering Allies

The witch's prophecy weighed heavily on Finn's mind as he made his way back toward the castle. Three trials lay before him, each a test of courage, wisdom, and grace. While the nature of the trials remained a mystery, one thing was clear: he could not face this journey alone. He would need allies—those with skills beyond his own, and who might help him survive whatever challenges lay ahead.

The first light of dawn was creeping over the horizon when Finn reached the outskirts of the castle's lower town. The cobbled streets were still and empty, shops closed and windows shuttered. He knew that most people wouldn't risk being outside until the sun was fully up, especially with rumours of strange happenings at the castle.

Finn's mind was racing with memories of people he had seen around the castle—figures that moved in the shadows, yet each with a reputation for unique talents. He decided to start with someone he'd heard of but never met directly: Roderic, a notorious thief with a reputation for slipping into places no one else could reach.

Finn found Roderic hiding in an abandoned alleyway near the castle walls. Roderic was a wiry young man with a quick smile and quicker hands, always lurking near the edges of trouble, though he was careful not to get caught. Finn had seen him around the market a few times, and though they'd never spoken, Roderic's reputation was well-known among the squires.

"Roderic," Finn called softly, peering into the shadows where he suspected the thief might be hiding.

The figure leaning against the wall straightened, his eyes narrowing as he recognized Finn. "A squire, looking for me? That's a first." Roderic grinned, crossing his arms. "You lost, kid?"

Finn took a breath, steadying himself. "I need your help."

Roderic raised an eyebrow, his interest piqued. "My help? What would a squire need from a thief?"

"I'm on a mission to find the king's lost crown," Finn said, deciding there was no point in hiding the truth. "If I don't recover it before dawn, the kingdom will fall under a curse."

Roderic's smirk faded, replaced by a thoughtful look. "The king's crown, eh? Sounds like a job with high stakes." He eyed Finn carefully, sizing him up. "What's in it for me?"

Finn had expected this question and pulled a small pouch from his cloak, one he had snatched from the castle's provisions before leaving. He opened it, revealing a handful of golden coins—the last of his savings, his reward for years of service as a squire. It was all he had.

"Help me, and it's yours," Finn said, holding the pouch out to him.

Roderic's eyes gleamed at the sight of the gold, but he hesitated, his gaze shifting from the coins to Finn's face. After a moment, he reached out and took the pouch, slipping it into his cloak. "Alright, squire. You've got yourself a deal. But know this—I'm only in it for the gold. Don't expect me to stick around for heroics."

Finn nodded. "That's all I need. Just help me get through places I can't reach on my own."

With Roderic's agreement, they set off to find the second person on Finn's list: Isadora, a young mage-in-training. Finn had only seen her once or twice in the castle gardens, where she practiced her magic under the careful eye of her mentor, a reclusive scholar known for studying arcane arts. Isadora was rumoured to be a prodigy, gifted with raw magical talent, though her powers were still in their early stages.

They found Isadora in the gardens, her face illuminated by the faint glow of a spell she was practicing, her focus unwavering. When she finally noticed them, her eyes widened in surprise at the sight of the squire and the thief.

"What are you two doing here?" she asked, her voice cautious.

"I need your help," Finn explained, once again recounting the urgent situation. He told her of the prophecy, the missing crown, and the curse that threatened to befall the kingdom by dawn.

Isadora's initial wariness softened as she listened. "You're serious about this, aren't you?"

Finn nodded, his face earnest. "I can't do it alone. The prophecy speaks of trials that will test courage, wisdom, and grace. I need someone with magical knowledge, someone who can help me understand the mysteries we might encounter."

Isadora hesitated, her gaze flickering to Roderic, who was leaning casually against a tree, clearly uninterested in the grandiosity of their quest. She looked back to Finn, her expression thoughtful. "I'm still in training. I can't perform powerful spells like my mentor, and some of the magic I know is... unpredictable."

"That's fine," Finn replied quickly. "Any magic at all could make the difference."

After a moment of silence, she gave a slow nod. "Alright, I'll join you. But only because the fate of the kingdom is at stake. This isn't just a simple favour, after all."

With a thief and a mage at his side, Finn felt a growing sense of hope. However, he knew he needed one more ally—someone experienced, someone who could guide them through the dangers they would surely face. That person, he realized, was Sir Cedric, a retired knight who had once served as the king's most trusted protector.

Sir Cedric lived in a small, quiet cottage on the outskirts of the castle grounds, having stepped away from his duties after a debilitating injury. He had trained many of the younger knights in his prime, and Finn knew that if anyone could help them navigate the challenges ahead, it was him.

When they reached the cottage, Sir Cedric was in his small garden, tending to a row of herbs. He looked up as they approached, his stern face softening slightly at the sight of Finn.

"Finn, what brings you here at such an hour?" he asked, wiping his hands on a cloth.

Finn took a deep breath and explained everything: the missing crown, the prophecy, the curse, and the trials he was destined to face. Cedric listened silently, his face growing grave as Finn spoke.

When Finn finished, the old knight remained silent for a long moment, his gaze distant. Finally, he looked at Finn, a hint of pride in his eyes. "The king chose well when he entrusted you with this mission," he said quietly. "I had my doubts about you, boy, but you've proven me wrong."

Finn looked down, his cheeks flushing slightly. "I need your help, Sir Cedric. You have the experience we lack, and I know you're the only one who can guide us through this."

Cedric gave a small nod, his expression resolute. "I may not be able to fight as I once did, but I can still wield a blade and offer counsel. And if Eldoria's safety depends on it, I will do what I can."

Roderic muttered under his breath, "Another knight... just what we need." But Finn ignored him, a feeling of reassurance washing over him. With Cedric's guidance, he knew they stood a better chance of surviving the trials ahead.

As the first rays of dawn stretched over the horizon, Finn looked around at his unlikely group of allies: a cunning thief, a mage still learning her powers, and a retired knight who had left his days of glory behind. They were a ragtag bunch, hardly a shining band of heroes, yet each of them held a skill or strength he would need.

"Thank you," Finn said, his voice steady. "We have until dawn tomorrow to retrieve the crown and save the kingdom. I won't pretend this will be easy, but I believe we can succeed together."

They nodded, each one holding a determined look, ready to face the unknown for reasons of their own. With the witch's prophecy guiding him, Finn led his newfound companions toward the forest path, where shadows stretched long and the air seemed to hum with mystery.

They were about to embark on a journey that would test their courage, their trust, and their very souls. The fate of Eldoria rested on their shoulders, and with his allies at his side, Finn felt the flicker of hope grow stronger. Together, they would face the trials, and perhaps, if they were worthy, recover the lost king's crown.

Chapter 7: The Prophecy's Map

As the group made their way into the forest, the early morning light filtered through the trees, casting a faint glow on the path ahead. Finn felt the weight of responsibility settle more heavily on his shoulders now that he had allies depending on him. Despite their varied backgrounds, each of them was committed to the mission in their own way. They moved quietly, senses alert, until they reached a clearing where they could pause and plan their next steps.

Finn was about to suggest they head deeper into the forest when a familiar presence washed over him—a chill in the air, as though the very forest held its breath. Out of the shadows emerged the witch, her robes blending seamlessly with the darkened forest, her silver hair shimmering faintly in the light. Finn and his companions froze, startled by her sudden appearance.

Isadora's eyes widened, her hand instinctively reaching for the amulet around her neck. Roderic shifted uncomfortably, muttering under his breath, "Is this the kind of company we're keeping now?"

The witch's piercing gaze silenced him, and her eyes softened as they landed on Finn. She nodded, as if satisfied that he had brought others to aid him. "You have gathered allies, young squire. Good. This task requires strength beyond your own."

Finn stepped forward, still somewhat awed by her presence. "We're ready to do what it takes. But we need your guidance."

A faint smile played on the witch's lips. "I knew you would return to seek me again." She reached into the folds of her cloak and pulled out a small, rolled parchment, its edges worn and frayed, the ink faded in some places yet still legible. Symbols and markings adorned the outside of the scroll, their shapes twisting like vines around an unseen center.

"This map," she said, holding it out, "will guide you on the path to the crown. But be warned—it does not mark a simple trail. It is written in riddles, and each clue leads to a place where a trial awaits you. Only by deciphering each step and facing the trials will you be able to reach the crown."

Finn took the map from her, feeling the ancient parchment rough beneath his fingers. He unrolled it carefully, his companions leaning in to study it with him. The map was unlike any he had ever seen. It was filled with cryptic symbols, words written in a language he didn't recognize, and strange, shifting images that seemed to move when he wasn't looking directly at them.

Isadora's brow furrowed as she examined the map. "This... it's not a normal map. Some of these symbols are ancient, maybe even pre-dating the kingdom itself."

The witch nodded. "These markings were made by those who understood the magic of the land, the deep power woven into Eldoria's soil and rivers. Only those who truly wish to restore the kingdom may read its secrets."

Cedric, the retired knight, studied the map with a frown. "This will take more than just a keen eye. These markings are riddles in themselves."

Roderic, however, seemed intrigued. "So, we just have to solve these little puzzles and follow the map? Doesn't sound too bad." But despite his light-hearted tone, his gaze lingered on the strange markings, revealing a hint of uncertainty.

The witch gestured to a specific part of the map, where a faint inscription had begun to glow, casting a soft light over the parchment. "This is where you begin," she said. "The riddle reads:

'In the forest's heart, where waters meet,
A shadow hides the wayward's seat.
Seek not the light but darkest shade,
Where ancient roots and secrets fade.'

Isadora traced the symbols with her finger, eyes narrowed. "It sounds like it's leading us to a place where rivers or streams intersect... perhaps where they pass under the canopy of ancient trees."

Finn nodded, remembering a spot just like that within the forest. "There's an old glade deep within these woods, where two streams converge beneath a grove of massive oaks. I've heard it's one of the oldest parts of the forest."

The witch's expression darkened, and she lifted her gaze to meet each of theirs in turn. "The path to the crown is filled with peril, and the map will only reveal as much as you are ready to know. Trust in each other, for the trials are meant to test not just your strength, but your loyalty, wisdom, and hearts. Many have tried to retrieve the crown before you, and none have returned."

Roderic scoffed lightly, though there was an edge to his tone. "So we're just walking into a death trap. Great."

The witch's gaze sharpened, silencing him once more. "This is no trap, thief. It is a test—of the spirit and the soul. Only those pure in heart, willing to sacrifice for the kingdom, will succeed. Remember the prophecy I gave to you, Finn, and heed it well."

Finn swallowed, nodding. He knew the witch's warning wasn't an idle one. They were embarking on a journey that would test each of them, and not all of them might return unscathed.

"Thank you," he said, his voice steady. "We won't let you down."

The witch inclined her head, a hint of sadness in her expression. "May the light guide you, even in the darkest of shadows." With a final look at the group, she melted back into the forest, her form vanishing into the mist as quickly as she had appeared.

The group stood in silence, the weight of her words pressing down on them. Finn looked down at the map, determination hardening in his chest. They had the first riddle, and with each clue, they would move closer to the crown—and, if they succeeded, to the salvation of Eldoria.

"Let's move," he said, his voice filled with resolve. "We don't have much time before dawn. If this map is leading us to the first trial, we need to be ready for anything."

His companions nodded, each of them understanding the gravity of what lay ahead. With Roderic's cunning, Isadora's magic, Cedric's wisdom, and his own unshakable determination, Finn felt a glimmer of hope that perhaps, just perhaps, they might succeed where so many others had failed.

Together, they set off deeper into the forest, the map guiding them toward their first destination. Shadows danced around them, and the forest seemed to whisper of ancient secrets and dangers that lay in wait. As they walked, the words of the riddle echoed in Finn's mind, reminding him that this path would demand everything he had to give—and more.

The journey to the heart of the forest, where waters met and shadows lingered, had begun.

Chapter 8: Secrets in the Shadows

The group trudged deeper into the forest, the ancient trees casting a thick canopy overhead that dimmed the morning light. The forest seemed alive, whispering in a language Finn couldn't quite understand, as if the very land were aware of their presence. Each step felt heavier, weighted by the urgency of their mission and the mysterious dangers that awaited them.

Finn held the map tightly, his eyes tracing the cryptic symbols and riddles that guided their path. The witch's warning rang in his mind: Not all who seem enemies are foes, and not all allies are what they seem. The words had unsettled him, hinting at betrayals and dangers beyond the physical trials they would face. Could it be possible that someone in his group had motives beyond saving Eldoria?

His gaze drifted over each of his companions, considering them in a new light. Roderic walked ahead, light on his feet, eyes scanning the forest with the ease of someone used to hiding in shadows. Though the thief had agreed to help, his loyalty was bought with gold, and Finn knew that such loyalty was fragile. Roderic had joined for profit, not for love of the kingdom. What would happen if someone offered him a better deal?

Isadora followed just behind Roderic, her fingers resting on her amulet. Her brow was furrowed, her gaze thoughtful as she occasionally muttered soft words under her breath, practicing spells. She was a mage-in-training, yes, but she was also ambitious and intelligent. Finn knew little about her background, and while she had agreed to help him, he couldn't shake the feeling that she had secrets of her own.

Finally, there was Sir Cedric, the retired knight whose wisdom and experience had already proven invaluable. Cedric had once served as the king's closest protector, yet he had left the castle under a cloud of rumours and whispers. Finn respected the knight deeply, but he couldn't help but wonder what might have caused such a loyal warrior to walk away from his sworn duty.

Shaking his head, Finn chided himself. He needed to focus on the mission, not sow distrust among his allies. But even as he tried to clear his thoughts, a troubling question lingered: If there truly was a spy in the castle, was it possible that the traitor had managed to join his group, waiting for the perfect moment to sabotage their mission?

They reached a clearing where two streams met under a cluster of ancient oaks, just as the first riddle had described. The air was thick with the scent of moss and damp earth, and the sound of water bubbling over rocks filled the silence. Roderic crouched down by the water's edge, examining the surroundings with a practiced eye.

"This is the place, isn't it?" he murmured, glancing back at Finn.

Finn nodded, studying the map once more. The ink shimmered faintly, and new words seemed to form on the parchment as if responding to their location.

"Beneath the roots where shadows dwell,
Lies the tale no one will tell.
Speak aloud the ancient vow,
And shadows shall reveal the how."

Cedric frowned as he read the words over Finn's shoulder. "An ancient vow... that could mean any number of things. But there were oaths sworn long ago by the first kings, vows meant to protect the kingdom. Perhaps one of those is the key."

Isadora stepped closer, her brow furrowed. "It's risky. Ancient magic is fickle. If we say the wrong vow, we might set off a trap rather than unlock a path."

Roderic smirked, his eyes gleaming. "Oh, now we're worried about traps? I thought that's what knights and mages were for."

Finn shot him a sharp look. "Enough, Roderic. If we're going to get through this, we need to work together."

But even as he said it, he couldn't shake the gnawing feeling of distrust in his gut. Every glance, every whispered word felt like a potential betrayal waiting to unfold. Trust, he realized, was as much a test as any trial the witch had warned them about.

He took a deep breath, pushing the doubts from his mind, and stepped forward to face the ancient oak. Remembering one of the old vows he had heard in a story as a child, he spoke aloud, his voice steady and clear.

"By honour and courage, by blood and crown, I swear to defend the kingdom from shadow and strife."

A gust of wind swept through the clearing, rustling the leaves overhead. Shadows pooled at the base of the tree, twisting and writhing until they revealed a narrow passage between the roots, leading deep into the earth.

Roderic looked impressed, but he quickly masked it with a smirk. "Not bad, squire. Seems like you might be useful after all."

Ignoring the jab, Finn motioned for them to follow him into the passage. The path was narrow and dark, the walls lined with roots and damp earth. It felt as if they were descending into the heart of the forest itself, surrounded by secrets hidden from the light of day.

As they moved deeper, Finn's nerves tingled. He felt as though something—or someone—was watching them. It wasn't the witch, he was certain of that. This presence felt different, sinister, like an unseen enemy lurking in the darkness, waiting for them to slip.

The passage opened up into a small chamber, lit by a faint, eerie glow. In the center of the room stood a pedestal, atop which lay a small stone engraved with strange symbols.

Isadora's eyes widened. "This must be part of the first trial. The riddle said we'd find clues here."

Roderic stepped forward, eyeing the stone. "Let's grab it and get out. The longer we stay here, the more likely we're walking into a trap."

But as he reached for the stone, Cedric stepped in front of him, his expression firm. "Patience, thief. Not everything is as it seems."

A tense silence fell over the group, and Finn realized that distrust had already started to poison them. The shadows of doubt hung thick between them, and every word seemed to hold a hint of suspicion.

Taking a deep breath, Finn reached for the stone, his fingers brushing the cold surface. As he lifted it, a low rumbling filled the chamber. Shadows began to swirl around them, coalescing into ghostly forms with hollow eyes and sharp claws.

Roderic cursed, drawing a dagger, while Isadora raised her hands, magic crackling at her fingertips. Cedric moved in front of Finn, his stance defensive, his hand on the hilt of his sword.

The shadowy figures advanced, their voices whispering secrets and lies, their words seeping into Finn's mind, fuelling his doubts.

"Your allies are not what they seem…" one shadow hissed, its voice slithering into his thoughts.

Another figure turned its hollow gaze toward Roderic. "Will you betray them, thief? Gold is a fickle master."

A third shadow whispered to Isadora. "Power calls to you, mage. Why follow when you could lead?"

The shadows moved closer, their whispers intensifying, trying to sow division and discord. Finn clenched his fists, realizing that this was the first trial: a test of trust, designed to tear them apart from within.

"Don't listen to them!" Finn shouted, his voice cutting through the whispers. "They're trying to turn us against each other!"

His words seemed to shake his companions out of their trance, and together they pushed back against the shadowy figures. Isadora summoned a burst of light that scattered the shadows, while Cedric's sword cut through their dark forms, sending them retreating into the edges of the chamber.

One by one, the shadows faded, leaving the group breathless and shaken.

Roderic gave Finn a hard look, his expression unreadable. "Maybe you're right, squire. Maybe we need to trust each other if we're going to get through this."

Isadora nodded, her gaze steady. "They wanted us to doubt each other, to question our motives. But we can't let them win."

Cedric placed a reassuring hand on Finn's shoulder. "You showed true courage, Finn. You held us together when the darkness tried to break us."

Finn managed a small smile, relief flooding through him. He knew the witch's words were true—trust was their most precious weapon, and he would have to guard it fiercely.

With the stone in hand and the first trial conquered, Finn led his allies out of the chamber, their resolve strengthened. They had faced the shadows of doubt and come through as a team. But he knew that the journey was far from over, and that greater tests of loyalty and trust still lay ahead.

For now, though, they moved forward together, each of them bound by the knowledge that trust, however fragile, was all they had.

Act 2: The Trials Begin

Chapter 9: Crossing the Forbidden Forest

The Forbidden Forest loomed ahead like a dark ocean of trees, stretching as far as the eye could see. Thick, twisted trunks rose from the earth, their branches woven together to form a dense canopy that blocked out the sky. Shadows hung heavy between the trees, and an unnatural silence filled the air, as if even the forest itself knew that something dark and ancient lingered within.

Finn took a steadying breath. He had heard tales of the Forbidden Forest since childhood—stories of travellers who had lost their way, never to return, and of ghostly figures that moved among the trees, illusions that lured wanderers deeper into the forest's clutches. But now, with the witch's map guiding him and his companions by his side, he pushed away the fear that whispered to him from the shadows.

They stood at the edge of the forest, each member of the group lost in their own thoughts. Cedric's hand rested on his sword hilt, his jaw set with quiet resolve. Roderic looked uneasy, his gaze darting from tree to tree, while Isadora's face was tense, her fingers tracing a protective rune on her amulet.

"Ready?" Finn asked, hoping his voice sounded more confident than he felt.

Roderic snorted, attempting to mask his nerves with a grin. "As ready as I'll ever be to walk into a haunted forest."

Cedric nodded, his voice calm. "Stay close, everyone. We don't know what lies within, but we'll face it together."

With that, they stepped into the forest, their footsteps muffled by the thick carpet of moss and leaves that covered the ground. The deeper they went, the darker the forest became. Sunlight struggled to pierce the thick canopy, and soon they were enveloped in shadows, the air thick and cold.

They walked in silence, each of them alert, their senses heightened by the oppressive stillness. Finn held the map tightly, his eyes scanning the faded markings for any hint of guidance. The symbols seemed to glow faintly, and he could make out the next part of the riddle:

"Through the woods where phantoms tread,
Find the path the lost ones dread.
Face the lies your mind will see,
And only then can you be free."

Finn's heart raced as he read the words aloud. "Face the lies your mind will see," he murmured, glancing around the forest. "I think the forest is going to try to deceive us."

Isadora nodded, her face thoughtful. "It means illusions, maybe spells meant to confuse us. We'll need to keep a strong grip on reality."

As if in response to her words, the trees around them seemed to shift, twisting into strange shapes. The shadows stretched and warped, forming eerie figures that swayed like wraiths in the dim light. Finn felt a strange pressure at the back of his mind, as though something were trying to creep in, to whisper lies and fears he couldn't quite hear.

They continued forward, but the path twisted in ways that made no sense. One moment, they were walking in a straight line, and the next, they found themselves back at the same moss-covered boulder they had passed minutes before.

"It's like the forest is moving around us," Roderic muttered, his voice tight with frustration.

Cedric placed a steadying hand on his shoulder. "Stay calm. Panicking will only make it worse."

They pressed on, but the forest continued to play tricks on them. Strange noises echoed through the trees—a woman's soft laughter, a child's faint cry, the sound of distant footsteps. Finn's head began to ache, and he felt the pull of something darker, like fingers reaching into his mind, trying to twist his thoughts and pull him into despair.

Then, through the mist, Finn saw a familiar figure standing just ahead, partially hidden among the trees. His breath caught in his throat as he recognized the face—it was his mother, her figure soft and ethereal, just as he remembered her from his earliest memories.

"Finn..." she called, her voice soft and warm. "Come closer, my boy. I've missed you."

He took a step forward, his heart pounding. His mother had been gone for years, taken by an illness that had left him orphaned. Yet here she was, smiling, her arms open, waiting for him.

"Finn, don't!" Isadora's voice cut through the haze, pulling him back to his senses. He blinked, and the figure vanished, replaced by a gnarled tree branch that resembled a figure only in his mind.

"It's the forest," she said, her voice tense but steady. "It's trying to lure us in, to make us lose ourselves in memories and illusions."

Finn nodded, shaken. He cast a wary glance at the shadows around him, realizing just how easily he had been pulled under the forest's spell.

They pressed forward, the illusions growing stronger with each step. Roderic stopped short, his face going pale as he saw something in the shadows, though he didn't speak of what he had seen. Cedric, too, was quiet, his hand gripping his sword as if it were his only anchor.

Suddenly, a new figure appeared on the path ahead: a monstrous creature with eyes like burning coals, its teeth sharp and glistening. It towered over them, blocking their way, and for a brief, terrifying moment, Finn felt the urge to turn and flee.

Cedric, however, held his ground, his sword raised. "It's another illusion!" he shouted. "Hold your ground and don't give in to fear!"

The creature let out a deafening roar, its eyes locked onto Finn, and for a moment, he felt the crushing weight of its presence, as if it were real. But he forced himself to remember the witch's warning and the prophecy's words. This was just another test—a test of their courage, meant to break them.

Clenching his fists, Finn shouted, "You're not real! You're nothing but shadows!"

The creature flickered, its form wavering, and then it vanished, leaving only the echo of its roar behind. One by one, the illusions faded, the figures retreating into the mist, and the path became clear once more.

They walked on, their steps steady, though the weight of what they had faced lingered with them. Each of them had seen something, some shadow dredged up by the forest, meant to shake them to their core.

After some time, they reached a small clearing, where a stream wound through the trees, its water clear and cool. Exhausted from the ordeal, they stopped to rest, each of them lost in their own thoughts.

Roderic broke the silence, his voice subdued. "That... that thing we saw back there. I don't know what it was for each of you, but it... it knew things about me. Things I try to forget."

Isadora nodded, her face sombre. "The forest preys on our weaknesses. It tries to make us doubt ourselves, to question what we see and what we know."

Cedric looked at Finn, his gaze steady. "You led us through that, Finn. You reminded us of what was real, even when the forest tried to twist our minds."

Finn managed a small smile, grateful for Cedric's words. He had nearly been lost to his own illusion, but his friends had brought him back. And perhaps that was the key to surviving the forest's trials—relying on each other, trusting in the strength they shared.

As they prepared to continue, Finn unfolded the map once more. The ink shimmered, revealing the next riddle, its words both a promise and a warning.

"Where the branches twist and rivers fork,
A secret lies beyond the dark.
Only those who see with heart,
May find the way and dare to start."

Finn looked up at his companions, his resolve strengthened by the ordeal they had survived. The Forbidden Forest had tried to break them, to lure them into despair, but they had come through it stronger.

"Let's keep moving," he said, his voice filled with determination. "The forest hasn't beaten us yet."

With renewed courage, they left the clearing and ventured further into the shadows, each step carrying them closer to the crown—and to the trials that lay ahead, waiting to test them in ways they had yet to imagine.

Chapter 10: The Guardian of the Bridge

The Forbidden Forest gradually gave way to a rocky, uneven landscape, where thick trees thinned out and mist curled over the ground like ghostly tendrils. The air grew colder as Finn and his companions continued onward, and soon, the sound of rushing water reached their ears.

They emerged from the woods to find themselves at the edge of a wide, churning river. In the center of the river stood a sturdy stone bridge, arched and covered with a thick layer of moss. But what truly caught their attention was the hulking figure standing squarely in the middle of it.

The creature was massive, with skin as grey and rough as the stones beneath its feet, a broad nose, and thick, crooked teeth protruding from its mouth. Its clothes were tattered rags, and in one hand, it clutched a long wooden club that looked as if it had been carved from an ancient tree. As the group approached, the creature's small, beady eyes narrowed, and it let out a deep, gravelly voice that echoed over the river.

"Stop right there!" it bellowed. "None shall cross this bridge without answering my riddles. I am Grimnar, guardian of this bridge, and none pass without proving their wits. So, who among you dares to take the challenge?"

Finn exchanged a nervous glance with his companions. They had all heard stories of trolls who guarded bridges, demanding payment or solving riddles to allow travellers to cross. But this was no fireside tale; Grimnar was real, and his gaze was fixed on them with fierce, unwavering determination.

"Three riddles," Grimnar continued, his voice a slow rumble. "Answer them all, and I shall let you cross. Fail, and you shall be my next meal."

Roderic muttered under his breath, "Just our luck, getting stuck with a troll who thinks he's a riddle master."

Cedric shot him a warning glance. "Careful. We need to take this seriously."

Isadora took a step forward, addressing the troll with a calm, steady voice. "We accept your challenge, Grimnar. Give us your first riddle."

The troll grinned, showing a row of yellowed teeth, and leaned on his club as he spoke:

"I have cities, but no houses.

I have mountains, but no trees.

I have water, but no fish.

What am I?"

Finn frowned, his mind racing as he tried to piece together the answer. The riddle painted a picture of something vast, something that contained these elements but in an unusual way.

After a moment, Isadora's face lit up with realization. "A map!" she said confidently. "A map has cities, mountains, and water, but no houses, trees, or fish."

Grimnar's grin faded slightly, replaced with a look of mild disappointment. "Very well," he rumbled. "You have answered correctly. But the next riddle will not be so easy."

The troll straightened, and his eyes gleamed with a mischievous light as he recited the second riddle:

"Forward I am heavy, but backward I am not.

What am I?"

The group fell silent, each of them lost in thought. Roderic scratched his head, muttering to himself. "Forward... heavy? Backward... not?"

Cedric's brow furrowed as he pondered the strange phrasing of the riddle. Then, he glanced at Finn, a spark of understanding lighting his eyes. "It's the word 'ton,'" he said slowly. "Forward, it spells 'ton,' which is heavy. But backward, it spells 'not,' which is... well, not."

Finn's eyes widened, realizing the cleverness of the answer. "Yes! 'Ton' and 'not.'"

Grimnar grunted, his expression darkening. He shifted his weight, tightening his grip on the club. "Very clever, travellers. But you have one more riddle to face. Fail this, and the river shall claim you!"

He leaned forward, his voice low and ominous as he presented the final riddle:

"I can be cracked, made, told, and played.

What am I?"

The group exchanged uncertain glances, each of them wracking their brains for an answer. The words swirled in Finn's mind—cracked, made, told, played. It sounded familiar, like something from the stories he had heard as a child, yet the answer remained elusive.

Roderic suddenly snapped his fingers. "Wait—I think I know it!" He looked at the troll, a grin spreading across his face. "The answer is 'a joke.' A joke can be cracked, made, told, and played."

Grimnar's eyes narrowed, and for a tense moment, Finn feared that he might refuse their answer. But then, with a frustrated sigh, the troll lowered his club and stepped aside.

"Clever you are," Grimnar muttered, grudging respect in his tone. "You have answered all three riddles correctly. You may cross the bridge... for now."

The group exchanged relieved smiles as they stepped onto the bridge, careful not to meet the troll's gaze. As they passed him, Grimnar watched them with a glint of something unreadable in his eyes, perhaps a hint of respect or perhaps the knowledge of more dangers ahead.

"Remember," he called after them, his voice echoing across the river, "not all trials are as simple as a riddle. Beware the road ahead, for it grows darker with every step you take."

With those final words, Grimnar turned and disappeared back into the shadows beneath the bridge, leaving them alone once more.

As they crossed to the other side, Finn felt a surge of confidence. They had faced the troll's challenge together, combining their strengths to solve the riddles. It was a reminder that each of them brought something unique to the group, and that their journey would demand all of their skills if they were to succeed.

They had passed the first of many trials, but Grimnar's parting words lingered in Finn's mind. The path ahead would only grow more treacherous, filled with dangers and choices that would test their hearts and minds in ways riddles could not.

With renewed determination, Finn led his companions onward, knowing that while they had conquered the bridge, their true journey was only beginning.

Chapter 11: The Squire's First Battle

The landscape beyond the bridge grew rugged and wild, with jagged rocks jutting from the earth and patches of thorny undergrowth that slowed their pace. Finn and his companions moved cautiously, aware that the dangers they faced might not only come from magical trials but from those who would go to any length to keep the crown hidden.

As they climbed a rocky hillside, the silence was broken by the snap of a twig. Finn froze, his hand tightening on the hilt of his sword. Shadows moved among the rocks above them, shifting and merging with the landscape. Then, without warning, a group of men emerged from the cover of the boulders, their faces hidden beneath hoods, each of them armed with a mix of swords and daggers.

Finn's heart pounded as he counted five bandits, their weapons gleaming in the pale light. Their leader, a burly man with a scar running down his cheek, stepped forward and smirked, his gaze cold and calculating.

"Seems we've caught ourselves a group of would-be heroes," the bandit leader sneered. "You're a long way from the castle, squire. And I don't imagine you'd have much need for that little map of yours if you're smart."

Finn squared his shoulders, trying to keep his voice steady. "We don't want any trouble. We're just passing through."

The bandit chuckled darkly. "Passing through? With a mission as important as yours?" He pointed his sword at Finn. "The crown belongs where it is. Turn back now, or you'll regret crossing our path."

Roderic tensed, his dagger ready, while Cedric stepped forward, his hand on the hilt of his sword, calm but alert. "If you want a fight, you'll find one here," Cedric said firmly. "But you'd be wise to reconsider."

The bandits ignored him, advancing with malicious grins. "Last warning, squire," the leader said, his eyes fixed on Finn. "Drop the map, and we'll let you go."

Finn felt a surge of defiance rise within him. These men had been hired to prevent anyone from finding the crown, likely by those who stood to gain from Eldoria's downfall. He couldn't turn back now, not when the kingdom's fate was at stake.

He drew his sword, feeling its weight in his hand, and glanced at Cedric, who nodded, his face proud. "Stand your ground, Finn. Trust your training."

The bandit leader sneered, lunging forward with a swing of his sword, his eyes glinting with malice. Finn's heart pounded, but he steadied himself, raising his blade to block the blow. Their swords clashed, the impact reverberating up Finn's arm, but he held his ground, pushing back with all his strength.

The bandit came at him again, faster this time, his movements fluid and practiced. Finn struggled to keep up, blocking and parrying with every ounce of skill he had learned as a squire. Each strike felt heavier than the last, and his arms began to ache, but he refused to back down.

Roderic and Isadora sprang into action as well, engaging two of the other bandits. Roderic moved with surprising agility, dodging attacks and landing quick strikes with his dagger, while Isadora muttered an incantation, her hands glowing as she cast a protective spell around them.

But Finn's focus remained on the leader, who sneered at him with a mixture of amusement and disdain. "Is this the best the king's squire can do?" the bandit taunted, driving his sword forward in a brutal thrust.

Finn sidestepped, barely dodging the blow, and struck back with a wild swing. The bandit blocked him easily, but Finn used the momentum to push forward, surprising his opponent with a quick jab to the side. The bandit staggered, momentarily thrown off balance, and Finn seized the opportunity, pressing the attack.

He remembered Cedric's teachings: move with purpose, defend only as long as needed, and look for an opening. Summoning all his courage, he dodged another strike and countered with a sharp, clean cut along the bandit's arm.

The leader let out a grunt of pain, his sneer fading into anger. He lunged forward, his strikes more frenzied now, and Finn realized he had made the fight personal. As the bandit's sword came down, Finn raised his own to parry, their blades locking.

The bandit sneered through gritted teeth. "You've got fire, boy. But fire burns out quick."

With a sudden burst of strength, Finn twisted his blade, breaking free of the lock, and delivered a quick strike to the bandit's knee. The leader stumbled, his balance wavering, and Finn followed through with a decisive blow to his shoulder, knocking him to the ground.

The leader glared up at him, clutching his wounded arm, his face twisted in pain and fury. "This isn't over," he hissed, backing away toward the edge of the clearing. "You may have bested me now, but you'll never reach the crown. Others will stop you... stronger than me."

He spat on the ground, then motioned to his men, who were already retreating. They vanished into the shadows, leaving Finn and his companions breathless and shaken but victorious.

Finn lowered his sword, his chest heaving as the reality of the fight settled over him. This had been his first true battle, a moment where his life—and the lives of his friends—had been on the line. And though his body ached, a flicker of pride warmed his heart. He had fought well, defending not only himself but the mission they all shared.

Cedric clapped him on the shoulder, his gaze approving. "Well done, Finn. You held your own, even against an experienced fighter. I'm proud of you."

Roderic, sheathing his dagger, raised an eyebrow with a smirk. "Not bad for a squire. I might just be glad you're with us."

Isadora smiled, her hand resting on her amulet. "Your courage saved us, Finn. That was brave."

Finn felt a surge of gratitude for their words, though he knew they all shared the victory. Together, they had faced the threat and emerged unscathed, their bond stronger for it. But the leader's parting words lingered in his mind, a dark reminder of the forces working against them.

"He mentioned others," Finn said, glancing at Cedric. "People who will try to stop us. Whoever stole the crown has gone to great lengths to make sure no one reaches it."

Cedric nodded, his face serious. "We must stay vigilant. These bandits were hired by someone with a vested interest in keeping the crown hidden. This is no small conspiracy."

With renewed resolve, Finn led his companions onward, their path now clearer but more dangerous than ever. He had fought his first battle and won, but he knew that this victory was only the beginning of a much larger struggle. Each step brought them closer to the crown, but also closer to the unknown enemies who lurked in the shadows, waiting to stop them at any cost.

As they continued through the rugged landscape, Finn's mind was sharper, his resolve hardened by the fight. He was no longer just a squire; he was a warrior, bound to protect his friends and his kingdom, no matter what awaited them on the path ahead.

Chapter 12: The Mysterious Merchant

The sun had begun its slow descent behind the trees as Finn and his companions reached a narrow, winding path through a dense forest. They were weary from the day's battles and trials, and their supplies were dwindling faster than Finn had anticipated. As they continued down the path, a strange smell wafted toward them—a mix of incense, herbs, and something unidentifiable but oddly inviting.

The smell grew stronger as they rounded a bend in the path, revealing a small, makeshift stall set up on the forest floor. Lanterns hung from branches overhead, casting a flickering glow on the array of oddities and trinkets displayed on a cloth-covered table. Behind the stall stood a man draped in dark robes, his face obscured by a wide-brimmed hat and a scarf wrapped around his mouth and nose. His eyes, sharp and gleaming, watched them with an intensity that sent a chill down Finn's spine.

"Well, well," the man said, his voice smooth and unsettling, as if he had been expecting them. "Travelers, so far from home. And on such an important quest, no less." He spread his arms wide, gesturing to his stall. "Welcome! I am Marden, a humble merchant with wares that might interest adventurers such as yourselves."

Cedric stepped forward, his gaze wary. "How do you know of our quest, merchant?"

Marden chuckled, his eyes narrowing with a glint of mischief. "Oh, I have my ways. Word travels fast, and whispers carry far in these woods. But let us not waste time with small talk. I have items that can aid you on your journey... for the right price, of course."

Roderic raised an eyebrow, smirking. "You've got a lot of nerve setting up shop in the middle of a forest. What's the catch?"

The merchant's gaze slid over to Roderic, a smile creeping behind his scarf. "No catch, my friends. Only opportunity. And besides, sometimes the most valuable treasures are found where least expected."

Finn's eyes drifted over the strange objects on the table: a vial of shimmering blue liquid, a small mirror with a cracked frame, an ancient-looking compass with strange symbols engraved on its face, and a black leather-bound book with no title. But it was a small, unassuming pendant that caught his attention. Its center held a single, faintly glowing stone, encased in an intricate silver design that seemed almost alive, as if it pulsed with its own heartbeat.

The merchant noticed Finn's interest and reached out, picking up the pendant with delicate fingers. "Ah, the Eye of Veilwood," he said, his voice soft and reverent. "A rare piece, indeed. This pendant holds a fragment of old magic, one that grants its wearer the Sight—the ability to see what lies hidden or obscured by illusions."

Finn's heart quickened. The forest and its trials had already deceived them once with illusions, and he had no doubt that more would await them on their path. This pendant could be exactly what they needed.

"Can it truly reveal illusions?" Finn asked, feeling the weight of the pendant's potential.

The merchant's eyes sparkled. "Oh, yes. It pierces through glamours, spells, even the shadows cast by one's own doubt. Wear it, and the truth will be laid bare before you."

Cedric frowned, his tone suspicious. "An artifact like that would come at a high price. What is it you're asking for?"

The merchant tilted his head, smiling beneath his scarf. "Not much, for such a powerful gift. I require something... meaningful, something that holds value to you beyond mere gold."

Finn hesitated, his gaze dropping to his side, where he kept a small leather pouch containing a pendant of his own. It was plain and simple, crafted by his mother before she had passed. It held no magical properties, only sentimental value—a reminder of home, of love, and of all he fought to protect. Parting with it felt impossible, but he understood that the merchant wanted more than just material wealth.

"You want something of personal value," Finn said slowly, understanding the price the merchant sought.

"Precisely," Marden said, his eyes glinting. "An object, a memory, a promise. It need only hold significance to you."

Roderic crossed his arms, muttering under his breath. "Sounds like a scam to me."

But Finn felt the tug of the pendant's promise. If this item could reveal the truth, then it was worth considering. The witch's prophecy had already warned of trials that would test their minds and hearts, and he knew that facing them blindly would only put his friends in greater danger. But to give up his mother's pendant... it felt like he would be losing a part of himself.

Isadora, noticing his inner struggle, placed a gentle hand on his shoulder. "Think carefully, Finn. The forest may hold more illusions, yes, but we also have each other. You don't have to do this."

Marden's gaze turned toward Isadora, and he gave a knowing smile. "True enough, young mage. But sometimes, even the strongest bonds cannot reveal the path that lies hidden."

Cedric watched the merchant with a wary eye. "Do not give him anything too dear, Finn. Trust that what you carry within is enough to see you through."

But Finn knew he couldn't shake the feeling that this pendant would be the key to something vital. With a deep breath, he reached into his pouch and pulled out his mother's pendant, the weight of it heavy in his hand. He held it out, hesitating one last time as memories of his mother's laughter and warmth flooded his mind.

"This," he said quietly, his voice thick. "This is my price."

Marden's eyes gleamed with satisfaction as he took the pendant, handling it as though it were a precious jewel. "A fair trade, indeed. Memories are powerful currency, young squire. They shape who we are, even as we leave them behind."

THE LOST KING'S CROWN

He handed the Eye of Veilwood to Finn, who took it with trembling hands, feeling its weight and the faint pulse of energy that emanated from within. As he slipped it over his neck, a strange clarity washed over him, as if the world had sharpened, each color brighter, each sound clearer. He felt an odd sense of loss mingled with strength, as though his mother's memory would now live within him, no longer bound to an object.

The merchant gave a slight bow. "May it serve you well. And remember, the power of sight can reveal truths, but it can also show you things you may not wish to see."

Without another word, Marden turned and vanished into the shadows of the forest, his stall gone as if it had never been there, leaving only the faint scent of incense and herbs behind.

Finn looked down at the Eye of Veilwood, feeling its warmth against his chest. He knew the cost had been steep, but he hoped it would be worth it in the trials ahead.

Roderic shook his head, muttering, "We'd better hope that thing works, or you just paid a king's ransom in memories."

Cedric gave Finn a reassuring nod. "You made a sacrifice. That takes courage, and it proves your commitment to this mission. Remember, Finn, your mother's spirit is with you, pendant or no pendant."

Finn managed a small smile, grateful for Cedric's words. With the Eye of Veilwood in his possession, he felt both a new strength and a new vulnerability, as if he had left a piece of himself behind in exchange for something unknown.

They set off once more, with Finn at the lead, his gaze sharper and more attuned to the shadows around them. He knew that the pendant would reveal more than illusions; it would reveal truths hidden from the eye and heart. As they continued on their journey, Finn vowed to make the most of his sacrifice, to ensure that his mother's memory would guide him to victory.

The road ahead was filled with unknown dangers, but with the Eye of Veilwood and his loyal companions by his side, he felt a renewed resolve. He would see this journey through, for his mother, his kingdom, and the crown that could save them all.

Chapter 13: The Valley of Echoes

As dusk settled, Finn and his companions reached the edge of a desolate expanse known as the Valley of Echoes. A sharp, biting wind whistled through the valley, carrying with it faint murmurs that seemed to drift in and out of hearing, like whispers just beyond the edge of thought. The air felt heavy, thick with an ominous energy that made the hairs on the back of Finn's neck stand on end.

The valley stretched before them, flanked by steep cliffs on either side, casting long shadows that danced and shifted with the setting sun. A narrow path wound through the valley floor, leading to the opposite side where their journey continued. But the closer they stepped toward the valley's mouth, the more Finn felt an unseen force pulling at him, clawing at his thoughts.

Roderic let out a low whistle. "So, this is the infamous Valley of Echoes. I've heard tales of travellers losing their minds here, haunted by... well, by something."

Cedric's expression was grim. "They say this valley remembers every fear, every doubt that has ever crossed it. Be on guard. This place will test us."

Finn felt a chill pass over him as he touched the Eye of Veilwood hanging around his neck. He had hoped the pendant might protect him from the valley's tricks, but he sensed that this place was different from the illusions in the forest. This was a trial that would reach deep into their minds, dredging up their fears and insecurities in ways they might not be prepared to face.

Isadora took a steadying breath. "The valley's magic feeds on our thoughts. Whatever we face here, we have to remember what's real. We're here together, and we can't let the whispers turn us against each other."

As they began their descent into the valley, the whispers grew louder, still fragmented but forming faint, almost recognizable words.

Each step seemed to amplify the voices, their words twisting in tone from soft and persuasive to dark and taunting.

Finn heard a voice, soft and familiar, winding through his mind. It was his mother's voice, but instead of the warmth he remembered, it held a tone of reproach.

"You think you can save the kingdom, Finn? You're just a squire, a boy playing at bravery. This task is beyond you."

He clenched his fists, forcing himself to ignore the words, but the whispers only grew louder, winding into every corner of his mind.

Roderic's face had turned pale, his normally light-hearted expression replaced by one of tense concentration. His eyes darted around, as though he were trying to shake off the weight of invisible accusations. "They're... they're saying things that aren't true," he muttered, though his voice was uncertain.

Cedric put a reassuring hand on Roderic's shoulder. "Stay focused. This valley is trying to unravel us. It wants us to doubt ourselves, to question our purpose."

The words helped, but only briefly, as a new wave of whispers rolled through the valley, this time directed at Cedric himself.

"You failed the king once, didn't you?" the voice sneered, its tone dark and mocking. "You think this mission will redeem you, old man? You're nothing but a relic, clinging to past glories."

Finn saw Cedric's jaw tighten, his eyes darkening as he visibly fought against the voice. The weight of the accusation seemed to settle heavily on his shoulders, but after a moment, he lifted his head, his gaze steely. "I know who I am," he whispered, more to himself than to the others.

Isadora stumbled, her hand going to her forehead as if she were in pain. Her face was pale, her expression torn between fear and frustration. Finn moved to steady her, but she waved him off, her voice trembling. "They're... they're saying I don't have control. That I'll fail you all when you need me most."

Her words struck Finn to his core. This valley, this cursed place, was somehow drawing out their deepest insecurities, the fears they hid even from themselves. It was like a mirror, reflecting the darkest parts of their hearts, showing them the things they tried to keep buried.

And then, as if sensing his own dread, the voices turned on him.

"Finn, you are nothing without your friends, a mere squire with no power, no experience," the voice taunted, mocking and bitter. "You think you can save Eldoria? You can't even save yourself."

The words cut deep, filling him with a sense of inadequacy that he couldn't easily push aside. Part of him wanted to believe the voice, to turn back and let someone more worthy take on this quest. But then he looked at his friends, all of them struggling against their own doubts and fears, yet standing by his side. If he gave in, he would be giving up not only on himself but on them as well.

He drew a shaky breath, clutching the Eye of Veilwood. "We have to keep moving," he said, his voice louder than the whispers. "We're here together, and we're stronger than these voices. They're lies, meant to turn us against ourselves and each other."

Cedric nodded, his expression resolute. "Finn's right. This valley is only as powerful as we allow it to be. We know who we are. We know why we're here."

Roderic's face softened, some of the tension leaving his posture. "Well, if you're all sticking around, I suppose I will too. Can't let you have all the fun."

Isadora managed a small, determined smile. "They may know our fears, but they don't know our strength."

With newfound resolve, they pushed forward, each of them holding tight to the truths that anchored them. The whispers continued, venomous and unyielding, but the words no longer held the same power. Finn reminded himself of his purpose, of the king's last command and the witch's prophecy, of the faith his friends had in him.

The path wound deeper into the valley, and though the air grew colder and the shadows lengthened, their steps did not falter. They moved as one, supporting each other when the whispers grew too strong, reminding each other of the bonds that held them together.

Finally, they reached the far end of the valley, where the cliffs opened into a sunlit glade. As they stepped out of the shadows, the whispers faded, replaced by the soft rustling of leaves and the warmth of daylight. It felt as if they had broken free from a weight that had been dragging them down, a darkness that clung to them but could not conquer them.

Finn let out a breath he hadn't realized he'd been holding, relief flooding through him. He looked at his companions, each of them worn but standing tall, their eyes filled with a shared determination.

Cedric clapped Finn on the shoulder, his voice filled with pride. "You led us through that, Finn. You reminded us of what mattered most."

Isadora nodded, her gaze steady. "Thank you, Finn. If you hadn't been there, I might have lost myself in those whispers."

Even Roderic managed a genuine smile. "Not bad for a squire, eh?"

Finn smiled, warmth blooming in his chest. "We made it through together. None of us could have done this alone."

They continued onward, the Valley of Echoes behind them, and a stronger bond forged among them. The valley had tested them in ways that no sword or spell could, probing into the parts of themselves they tried to hide. But they had emerged stronger, unshaken in their resolve to reclaim the crown and save Eldoria.

As they pressed on, Finn knew that more trials lay ahead, and that the road would only grow darker. But he also knew that, no matter what the whispers had said, he was not alone. Together, they were a force that no valley of shadows could conquer. They had faced their fears—and they were ready for whatever lay ahead.

Chapter 14: The Trapped Shrine

The sun was low in the sky by the time Finn and his companions reached the base of a rocky hillside, where the remnants of an ancient shrine stood, half-hidden by creeping vines and layers of moss. Stone pillars, worn by centuries of wind and rain, flanked the entrance, each carved with faded runes and symbols that hinted at the shrine's forgotten power. At the center, an arched doorway led into darkness, a yawning portal to whatever secrets lay inside.

Finn felt a shiver of anticipation as he looked at the shrine. This place, though silent and still, seemed to hold a presence, an energy that was both inviting and foreboding. He knew, deep down, that they were close to something vital, a clue that might guide them further on their quest for the crown.

Isadora stepped forward, studying the carvings on the stone pillars. "These symbols... they're ancient, older than even the oldest records I've read. This shrine may have been built by the same people who crafted the crown."

"Then it makes sense that there would be a clue hidden here," Cedric said, his eyes narrowed as he scanned the doorway. "But something tells me it won't be easy to retrieve."

Roderic smirked, adjusting his daggers. "If it were easy, everyone would have found the crown ages ago."

Finn nodded, stepping toward the entrance, his hand resting on the hilt of his sword. As he neared the doorway, a faint glimmer of light flickered within, illuminating a stone pedestal at the far end of the chamber. On the pedestal rested a small, ornate box, its surface inlaid with symbols similar to those on the pillars outside.

"That must be it," Finn murmured. "Whatever clue we're meant to find is inside that box."

He took a cautious step forward, but Cedric placed a firm hand on his shoulder, stopping him. "Wait. This shrine may be ancient, but I'd wager it's well-protected. We need to be careful."

Roderic gave a small, approving nod. "For once, I agree with the old knight. Shrines like these are usually riddled with traps. It's practically tradition."

Isadora cast a spell, her hands glowing softly as she murmured an incantation. A faint shimmer spread over the floor, revealing a series of hidden pressure plates embedded in the stone. "There," she said, pointing. "Those plates will trigger something if we step on them. We'll have to move carefully."

Roderic grinned, his eyes gleaming with excitement. "This is where I come in. Watch and learn."

With surprising agility, Roderic slipped forward, weaving between the pressure plates with practiced ease. He paused near the center of the room, glancing back at them with a smirk. "Simple enough. Just follow my lead and avoid stepping on the plates."

Finn, Cedric, and Isadora followed Roderic's path, each of them moving carefully to avoid triggering the traps. But as they neared the pedestal, a faint hum filled the air, and a section of the wall slid open, revealing a line of small, sharpened darts poised to fire.

Roderic's smirk vanished. "Well, that's new."

The darts shot forward in rapid succession, forcing them to duck and dodge as the projectiles embedded themselves into the stone floor around them. Finn's heart raced as he narrowly avoided a dart that whizzed past his ear, embedding itself in the wall with a deadly thud.

Isadora raised her hands, casting a protective shield around them. The darts clattered harmlessly against the magical barrier, but the strain showed on her face as she maintained the spell. "Hurry... I can't hold this for long!"

With Isadora's shield giving them a brief respite, Finn and Roderic moved closer to the pedestal. But as they did, a second trap triggered:

the floor began to shift, the tiles rearranging into a twisting pattern beneath their feet. Some sections of the floor fell away, revealing deep pits lined with jagged spikes.

"Careful!" Cedric shouted, steadying himself as the ground shifted.

Finn's heart pounded as he balanced on the narrow ledge of stone, glancing down at the deadly spikes below. He could see the box, tantalizingly close but separated by a stretch of treacherous, shifting ground.

"Isadora, any ideas?" Finn called, struggling to maintain his balance.

She bit her lip, concentration etched on her face. "There's too much magic layered into these traps. Disabling them could take hours we don't have. I might be able to freeze the floor momentarily, but it will be risky."

Cedric nodded. "Do it. We'll cover you."

Isadora muttered another incantation, extending her hands toward the ground. A wave of frost spread from her fingertips, coating the floor in a thin layer of ice. The shifting tiles slowed, freezing in place for a brief moment.

"Now!" she urged, her voice strained.

Finn took a deep breath, then leapt across the frozen tiles toward the pedestal, his feet slipping slightly on the ice but managing to stay balanced. He reached the pedestal, his heart racing as he reached out to grab the box.

But the moment his fingers touched it, a final trap activated. The ceiling above him rumbled, and a heavy stone slab began to descend, its weight casting a shadow over Finn.

"Finn, move!" Cedric shouted, reaching out to pull him back.

Finn snatched the box from the pedestal, tucking it securely under his arm. He leapt backward just as the stone slab slammed into place, narrowly missing him. He stumbled, catching himself before tumbling into one of the spiked pits.

With the box in hand, he made his way back to his companions, who were all watching him with a mix of relief and admiration.

"Well done, squire," Cedric said, clapping him on the shoulder. "That was no small feat."

Roderic grinned, giving Finn an approving nod. "Not bad for your first real heist."

Isadora lowered her hands, the frost on the floor melting as the magic dissipated. She looked exhausted, but managed a smile. "Now, let's hope the contents of that box were worth the trouble."

Finn held up the box, examining its intricate carvings. He carefully lifted the lid, revealing a small, rolled parchment tied with a thin strip of leather. His fingers trembled slightly as he unrolled it, revealing a series of symbols and a short, cryptic verse:

"Beyond the veil where shadows fall,

Seek the truth within the hall.

A heart of courage, pure and strong,

Will find the place where you belong."

Finn read the words aloud, feeling a strange mixture of excitement and foreboding. The clue seemed to hint at their next destination, but the meaning was still shrouded in mystery.

Isadora frowned, studying the parchment. "This 'hall' could be anywhere. But I think the verse is telling us that we'll need courage—and perhaps something more—to find the crown."

Cedric nodded, his gaze thoughtful. "If our journey so far has taught us anything, it's that each trial is a test of not only our strength, but of our hearts and minds. This next part of the path may demand more from us than anything we've faced yet."

Roderic rolled his eyes, though a hint of unease flickered in his expression. "Great. More ominous verses. Just what we needed."

But Finn felt a growing sense of purpose as he held the parchment. Each step brought them closer to the crown, and to the salvation of

Eldoria. No matter how dangerous the trials became, he knew they had the strength to face them.

They left the shrine, moving back into the forest with the riddle fresh in their minds. Whatever dangers awaited them next, Finn felt ready. He had braved the shrine's traps, unlocked another piece of the puzzle, and emerged stronger for it.

And with his friends by his side, he knew they were prepared to face whatever awaited them beyond the veil.

Chapter 15: Nightfall at Black Hollow

By the time the group reached Black Hollow, the sun had disappeared behind the mountains, leaving the sky painted in hues of purple and grey. Black Hollow was a village shrouded in legend and rumour, a place most travellers avoided for fear of the curse that had long settled over it. Stories told of villagers who had vanished overnight, leaving their homes untouched, as if they had simply melted into the shadows.

The houses in Black Hollow stood crooked and empty, their windows dark and hollow like empty eyes staring at Finn and his companions as they entered. The air felt thick and heavy, filled with a silence that was almost unnatural. It was as if the village itself was holding its breath, watching and waiting.

"This place gives me the creeps," Roderic muttered, his eyes darting to the shadows between the houses. "I'd rather sleep under the stars than in this ghost town."

Cedric shook his head, scanning the village. "We need shelter. Black Hollow may be cursed, but the night grows colder, and there's no better option nearby."

Isadora nodded, though her expression was troubled. "I've heard of places like this. Places touched by dark magic, where fears come alive. We'll need to stay close and keep our minds focused."

As they moved further into the village, the hairs on the back of Finn's neck prickled, as though something unseen were watching them from the darkness. Each house looked more foreboding than the last, their doors slightly ajar, as if beckoning the travellers inside. Finn could almost hear a faint whisper on the breeze, calling his name, filling him with an urge to turn back, to leave Black Hollow before something terrible happened.

They found a small, abandoned inn near the village center. It looked slightly less decayed than the other buildings, with a sturdy roof and a single, flickering lantern hanging from the front porch. Inside, the air was stale, but the tables and chairs were still intact, and the fireplace held remnants of wood that, with some effort, Cedric managed to coax into a low, crackling flame.

They settled in near the fire, their faces lit by its orange glow, but the warmth did little to dispel the chill that seemed to permeate the very walls of the inn. The silence was heavy, filled only by the occasional crackling of the fire and the distant creak of wooden beams settling.

Roderic broke the silence with a forced chuckle. "Well, it could be worse, right? At least we have walls and a roof."

But his attempt at humour fell flat, the oppressive atmosphere weighing down on them all. Finn wrapped his cloak around himself, fighting off the unease that settled like a stone in his stomach.

As they sat by the fire, an odd sensation began to creep over Finn. He felt... observed, as though the shadows in the corners of the room were growing eyes, watching his every move. He glanced around, trying to shake off the feeling, but then he saw something out of the corner of his eye—a figure, faint and flickering, standing by the doorway.

It was his father.

Finn's heart skipped a beat. His father had died when he was very young, but he remembered that face, the strong, proud man who had lifted him onto his shoulders as a boy, who had taught him to hold a wooden sword and pretend to be a knight. But there was something wrong. His father's face was twisted, eyes empty and filled with sadness.

"Finn," the apparition whispered, his voice low and hollow. "Why did you leave me?"

Finn felt frozen, unable to tear his gaze away from the ghostly figure. "I... I didn't," he stammered, his voice barely more than a whisper. "I—"

Isadora placed a hand on his shoulder, snapping him back to reality. "Finn, there's nothing there. It's an illusion. Black Hollow is trying to break you."

The figure of his father faded, melting into the shadows as if it had never been there. Finn swallowed hard, his hands trembling. The curse of Black Hollow was more insidious than he'd imagined. It was not merely an illusion; it was a weapon, wielded against their deepest fears.

Nearby, Roderic was muttering to himself, his face pale as he stared into a dark corner of the room. "I didn't mean to betray you... I had no choice. They left me no choice." His eyes were wide with terror, fixed on something none of them could see.

Cedric grabbed Roderic's shoulder, shaking him gently. "It's not real, Roderic. Focus on the here and now. Whatever you're seeing, it's in your mind. It's the curse of this place, trying to twist your thoughts."

Roderic blinked, snapping out of his trance, his breath coming in shallow gasps. "I... I know. But it felt so real. Like a shadow from my past, rising to haunt me."

Isadora, too, seemed shaken, though she had closed her eyes, whispering a protective spell under her breath to ward off whatever phantoms haunted her thoughts. Cedric, ever stoic, kept his gaze on the fire, his face a mask of quiet determination, though Finn could see the strain in his eyes. Whatever fears Cedric harboured, he was keeping them tightly controlled, unwilling to let them surface in this cursed place.

Finn drew a deep breath, his hand clutching the Eye of Veilwood. He could feel its faint pulse against his chest, grounding him, giving him the strength to resist the illusions. He remembered the witch's warning, that they would face trials that tested their hearts and minds, and he realized that Black Hollow was one such trial, a place where only the strongest of will could pass unscathed.

"We can't let this place get to us," Finn said, his voice steady. "Black Hollow feeds on our fears, but those fears aren't real. They're only as powerful as we allow them to be."

Isadora nodded, drawing strength from his words. "You're right. This curse is meant to unravel us, to turn us against ourselves. We have to stay focused."

They huddled closer to the fire, each of them holding tightly to their own thoughts, fighting the whispers that drifted in and out of the silence like tendrils of smoke. Shadows danced around them, forming shapes that threatened to pull them into despair, but together they held their ground, reminding each other of their purpose, of the mission they had sworn to see through.

Hours passed, each one feeling longer than the last, until finally, the faint light of dawn crept into the room, casting the shadows away. The chill that had settled over the inn lifted, and the oppressive weight of Black Hollow's curse seemed to ease, replaced by a sense of relief and release.

Roderic let out a breath he hadn't realized he'd been holding. "I never want to come back here," he muttered, shaking his head.

Cedric managed a small, weary smile. "Agreed. But we made it through, and we're stronger for it."

Finn looked at each of his companions, feeling a renewed sense of gratitude and respect for them. They had faced the darkness of Black Hollow together, standing strong against their deepest fears, and they had emerged as a stronger, more unified team.

As they left Black Hollow behind, Finn felt a weight lift from his heart, as if he had shed a piece of the fear that had clung to him for so long. He knew that there would be more trials ahead, challenges that would test them even further, but he also knew that they would face them together.

And whatever lay ahead, he was ready.

Chapter 16: The Bandit Queen's Lair

After leaving Black Hollow, the path led Finn and his companions through dense woods and into the heart of a hidden valley, where rumours said a powerful bandit queen had established her lair. The Bandit Queen was known throughout the kingdom, not only for her ruthlessness and cunning but also for her collection of rare treasures and secrets. Finn had heard whispers that she dealt in information and held powerful objects that even the kingdom's nobles sought after—if they dared to seek her out.

They approached a massive wooden fort, hidden among the thick trees. Torches lined the walls, casting a flickering glow over the rough-hewn logs and stone towers. Guards stood at attention, their weapons glinting in the torchlight, watching every move as Finn and his companions were led through the gates. It was clear that the Bandit Queen did not tolerate weakness or fear within her walls.

Inside the fort, they were escorted to a large tent at the center of the camp, draped in vibrant red and gold fabrics. The air was thick with incense, mingling with the earthy smell of leather and metal. As they stepped inside, Finn's eyes adjusted to the dim light and focused on the figure seated on a carved wooden throne at the back of the tent.

The Bandit Queen was a tall woman, her dark hair woven with silver rings, and her sharp, dark eyes studied them with a mixture of amusement and curiosity. She wore leather armour, adorned with various talismans and charms, and a heavy necklace of intricate stones hung around her neck. She looked both regal and dangerous, every inch a queen in her own domain.

"Well, well," she drawled, her voice smooth but edged with steel. "The squire and his loyal band, come all the way to my humble abode. I can only assume you're here for something very important." Her eyes sparkled with intrigue as they settled on Finn. "I've heard whispers of your quest. Rumours travel quickly, even in these woods."

Finn stepped forward, keeping his voice steady. "We seek the crown of Eldoria. We believe you have a clue that can lead us to it."

The Bandit Queen raised an eyebrow, her lips curling into a slight smile. "Straight to the point, are we? I like that." She leaned back, studying him with a look that was both calculating and amused. "But I don't part with information so easily. My secrets come at a price, especially for those seeking something as valuable as the crown."

"What is it you want in return?" Cedric asked, his tone cautious.

The Bandit Queen's gaze shifted from Cedric to Finn, her smile widening. "I don't need gold or jewels. No, my price is something... more personal." She paused, her eyes locking onto Finn with a look that made him uneasy. "I want something that will test the very heart of this young squire."

Finn swallowed, his nerves on edge. "What kind of sacrifice?"

The Bandit Queen rose from her throne, circling him slowly, her gaze never leaving his face. "Your friends mean much to you, do they not?" she asked, her voice soft, almost coaxing. "You would risk your life for them, fight for them. And yet... loyalty comes with a cost."

Finn nodded slowly, unsure of where she was going with this. "I trust them with my life. They're more than friends—they're like family."

"Then here is my demand," she said, her voice hardening. "You will leave behind one of them. In exchange for the clue you seek, you must choose one of your companions to remain here in my service, bound by oath for one full year."

Finn felt his heart plummet. Leave behind one of his friends? The thought was unimaginable. They had fought together, faced their fears together, and grown stronger as a team. He couldn't abandon any of them, not when their mission depended on each other's strength.

"That's... that's impossible," he said, his voice wavering. "I can't choose. We need each other."

The Bandit Queen's smile faded, replaced by a look of cold, unyielding resolve. "Then you don't want the crown badly enough, do you? A true leader knows that sacrifice is sometimes necessary, even if it means abandoning those closest to him."

Roderic shifted uncomfortably, glancing at Finn. "You don't have to do this, Finn. We'll find another way."

But the Bandit Queen shook her head, her gaze unwavering. "This is the only way. Choose someone, or leave here with nothing."

Finn's mind raced, torn between his loyalty to his friends and the importance of their mission. He couldn't imagine leaving any of them behind. Each one of them had brought him through the trials so far—Cedric with his guidance and wisdom, Isadora with her knowledge of magic, and Roderic with his agility and courage. They were a team, and each of them was essential to finding the crown.

But then he remembered the prophecy, the reminder that he would face trials that tested not just his courage but also his loyalty and heart. And he realized that this choice was one of those tests—a test of whether he would put his own needs above those of his friends.

After a long, agonizing silence, Finn looked up at the Bandit Queen, meeting her gaze with determination. "If it's a sacrifice you want, then take me instead," he said, his voice steady. "I'll stay and serve you for a year if you'll let my friends go and give them the clue they need."

The Bandit Queen's expression softened, and a flicker of respect appeared in her eyes. She regarded him silently for a moment, as if weighing the sincerity of his words. "You would truly give yourself up to serve me, just to spare your friends?"

Finn nodded, feeling the weight of his decision settle over him. "Yes. They need to complete this quest, with or without me. If staying here means they can find the crown, then I'm willing to do it."

A murmur of surprise and admiration passed through his companions, each of them looking at him with a mixture of pride and disbelief.

The Bandit Queen let out a low, amused chuckle. "Well, I must admit, I didn't expect that answer." She tilted her head, studying him with a new intensity. "Most who come seeking my help are willing to betray their own to achieve their goals. But you... you are willing to give up your own freedom for theirs."

She stepped back, crossing her arms. "Very well, squire. You have proven your worth, and your loyalty is clear. I'll give you the clue you seek, without demanding your sacrifice. But remember this: true loyalty is rare, and I do not give my gifts lightly. You may need this loyalty even more than you realize before your journey is over."

With a wave of her hand, she summoned one of her guards, who placed an ancient scroll in her hand. She passed it to Finn, her eyes glinting with amusement. "This scroll contains the next piece of your puzzle. Use it wisely."

Finn took the scroll, relief flooding through him. He opened it, scanning the words written in elegant, faded script:

"In the darkened hall where secrets lie,
Look not with sight but with your mind's eye.
The path is hidden, bound by grace,
Only the selfless will find the place."

The words resonated with him, a new mystery unfolding within his mind. He closed the scroll and looked up at the Bandit Queen, offering her a respectful nod. "Thank you. I won't forget this."

She gave him a faint smile, one that almost looked sad. "Remember, squire, there will come a time when you must choose again. And the next choice may not be as forgiving."

With that, she gestured for them to leave. Finn and his companions left the tent, the weight of the Bandit Queen's warning settling over them like a shadow. They walked in silence until they were beyond the walls of the bandit camp, the forest around them dark and quiet.

Cedric placed a hand on Finn's shoulder, his gaze filled with pride. "What you did back there... it took courage. You showed true leadership, Finn."

Isadora nodded, her eyes soft. "Sacrificing yourself to save us was the bravest thing you could have done. Thank you."

Roderic smirked, though there was admiration in his eyes. "I wouldn't have let you go, you know. But it was a noble offer."

Finn managed a small smile, his heart filled with gratitude for his friends. He had passed the Bandit Queen's test, but he knew that her words held a truth he couldn't ignore. More choices lay ahead, and each one would test him in ways he could not yet imagine.

For now, though, they had the next clue. And with his friends beside him, Finn felt ready to face whatever trials awaited them on their journey to reclaim the lost crown.

Act 3: Into the Depths

Chapter 17: The Druid's Secret

The journey to the Druid's Grove took Finn and his companions deep into the heart of the forest, to a place untouched by time or human hands. The trees were ancient, their trunks twisted and gnarled, and the air seemed thick with magic, humming with life and secrets older than the kingdom itself. Finn had heard tales of the druids, mysterious keepers of the land's magic, but he had never expected to meet one, let alone seek their guidance.

As they approached the grove, they saw him waiting—a tall, stooped figure cloaked in dark green robes, his white hair cascading down to his shoulders like a waterfall of moonlight. His face was lined with age and wisdom, his eyes sharp and penetrating as he watched them approach.

"Welcome, travellers," the druid said, his voice as deep as the forest itself. "I have been expecting you. Few seek the path you walk, and fewer still survive it."

Finn stepped forward, bowing his head in respect. "We seek the lost crown of Eldoria. We believe it is the key to saving the kingdom."

The druid nodded slowly, his gaze shifting to each of them in turn. "The crown... yes, it is no ordinary relic. Its magic runs deep, entwined with the very roots of this land. But you must understand—reclaiming the crown is not merely a matter of finding it. To wield it is to embrace its power, and that power comes with a price."

Isadora looked intrigued, her eyes shining with curiosity. "What do you mean? What kind of power does the crown hold?"

The druid gestured for them to sit in a circle on the moss-covered ground, and they obeyed, sensing that what he was about to reveal was of great significance. He reached into a pouch at his waist and pulled out a handful of crushed herbs, sprinkling them onto the ground. As he whispered a few words, the air shimmered, and a faint image appeared—a vision of a crown forged from silver and gold, set with gems that seemed to pulse with their own light.

"This crown," the druid began, his voice reverent, "was forged by the first mage-king, a man who bound his life force to the land. His intention was pure: to protect Eldoria from the forces of darkness. The crown was designed to channel the land's magic, to unite the king with his kingdom in body and soul. Whoever wears the crown wields not only authority but the magic of Eldoria itself."

The vision of the crown flickered, and Finn felt a strange pull toward it, as if he could feel the power it held even across time and space. But there was something dark within it as well, a weight that seemed to press down on his heart.

Roderic shifted uneasily, crossing his arms. "And what's the catch? I'm guessing this kind of power doesn't come without some sort of... complication."

The druid's gaze darkened. "Indeed. The magic of the crown binds the wearer to the kingdom, and in doing so, it slowly drains their life. Each king who has worn the crown has become a part of Eldoria, their life ebbing away over time until they are but a shadow, a memory in the land itself."

Cedric frowned, his face set in grim understanding. "So the crown doesn't just grant power—it takes something in return. The life of the king."

The druid nodded solemnly. "Yes. And that is why the crown was hidden. The last king could not bear the toll it took upon him, and so he entrusted it to those who would keep it safe until a true heir, willing to bear the weight of its power, would come forth. But with the crown lost, the kingdom suffers. The land weakens, and darkness gathers."

A tense silence fell over the group as they absorbed the druid's words. The crown was both a blessing and a curse—a tool of protection that demanded the ultimate sacrifice from those who dared to wield it.

Isadora's face was thoughtful, yet troubled. "If we find the crown, whoever wears it will be bound to Eldoria, sacrificing their own life to protect it. That's... that's not a decision to take lightly."

Roderic scoffed, though there was unease in his voice. "So you're saying whoever wants to rule Eldoria has to give up their life? Doesn't seem like much of a reward for saving the kingdom."

Finn felt a knot form in his stomach as he considered the druid's words. He had thought that retrieving the crown would be enough to save Eldoria, but he hadn't realized the true cost. If he were to find the crown and place it upon the king's head, that king would slowly fade, giving his life back to the land.

The druid's gaze shifted to Finn, his expression unreadable. "And what of you, young squire? Do you still seek the crown, knowing the price it demands?"

Finn hesitated, the weight of the question pressing down on him. He thought of the king's last command, the hope of restoring Eldoria to peace. But could he truly ask someone—perhaps even himself—to take on that burden, knowing the cost? He glanced at Cedric, Isadora, and Roderic, each of whom seemed lost in their own thoughts, grappling with the revelation in their own way.

After a long silence, he looked up, meeting the druid's gaze. "If the crown is what's needed to save Eldoria, then we have no choice. Someone has to bear it, to give their life so that the kingdom can live."

Cedric nodded, his eyes filled with quiet resolve. "Sacrifice is part of leadership. The needs of the many outweigh the needs of the few. If someone must take on that burden, then so be it."

But Isadora's face was filled with hesitation. "It's not that simple, Finn. Sacrifice may be necessary, but it's not something to accept blindly. Whoever bears the crown should choose that fate willingly, understanding what it means."

Roderic shook his head, his tone bitter. "I don't know about the rest of you, but this all sounds like madness to me. Giving up your life for a kingdom that doesn't even know you? For a crown that'll bleed you dry? Seems like a fool's bargain."

The druid watched their exchange, a faint smile on his lips. "Every person must decide for themselves what they are willing to give. True power lies not in the crown itself but in the choice to wear it."

Finn clenched his fists, feeling the tension building among them. He understood Roderic's reluctance; the idea of giving up one's life for the kingdom was terrifying. And yet, he also understood Cedric's sense of duty, Isadora's cautious approach, and the druid's wisdom.

The druid reached into his robe and pulled out a small stone, etched with intricate symbols. "Take this," he said, handing it to Finn. "It will guide you to the crown's resting place. But heed my warning: the final trial will test not only your courage but the purity of your intentions. Only one willing to sacrifice will find it."

Finn accepted the stone, feeling its cool weight in his palm. He looked up at the druid, determination flickering in his eyes. "Thank you. We'll take your warning to heart."

The druid nodded, his gaze softening. "May the wisdom of the land guide you, young squire. Remember, true strength lies in the heart, not in the crown. And when the time comes to choose, let that strength be your guide."

They left the grove, a heavy silence hanging over them as they returned to the forest path. The revelation of the crown's nature weighed on each of them, stirring a storm of emotions—fear, duty, and doubt.

Isadora finally broke the silence, her voice soft but steady. "Whatever happens, we'll face it together. No one has to carry this burden alone."

Cedric placed a hand on Finn's shoulder, his eyes filled with pride. "You have the heart of a leader, Finn. Whatever the cost, you'll make the right choice."

Roderic said nothing, his gaze fixed on the path ahead, his face unreadable. But Finn saw a flicker of something—perhaps respect, perhaps fear—in his eyes.

As they continued their journey, the weight of the crown's power and the sacrifice it demanded hung over them like a shadow. Finn knew that the final choice would come down to him, and he vowed that when the moment arrived, he would make that choice with courage, with wisdom, and, above all, with a heart willing to give everything for the kingdom he loved.

They were closer than ever to the crown's resting place, but Finn understood that the true test lay not in finding it, but in deciding who would bear its burden.

Chapter 18: The Whispering Woods

The Whispering Woods stretched before them, a seemingly endless maze of towering trees cloaked in mist. The air was thick with the scent of damp earth and moss, and a strange, almost musical whispering drifted through the trees, as if the forest itself were alive, humming a song only it could hear. Finn felt a chill as he stared into the depths of the woods. The stories he had heard about this place had been strange and unsettling—tales of travellers who had entered only to emerge changed, or never emerge at all.

The druid's words lingered in his mind: "Only the selfless will find the place." He wondered if the forest would put them to that test, if the Whispering Woods would force each of them to confront their intentions and loyalties.

They stepped forward cautiously, keeping close together. The fog seemed to thicken the deeper they went, swirling around their feet and rising up to their waists like a silvery river. The trees grew denser, their branches intertwining overhead to create a canopy that blocked out the light, casting everything in a dim, eerie glow.

"We stay close," Cedric said firmly, his voice low but reassuring. "This place is known to play tricks. Don't trust what you see."

But it was harder than it sounded. The whispers grew louder, weaving in and out of Finn's mind, soft and inviting, like a lullaby. As they walked, he began to hear faint voices, voices that sounded achingly familiar. He saw fleeting shapes in the mist, shadowy figures that seemed to call out to him.

"Finn..."

He froze, his heart pounding. It was his mother's voice, gentle and warm, the way he remembered it from his childhood. He turned, his gaze fixed on a figure standing in the shadows between two trees. It was her—her face soft, her eyes full of love, reaching out a hand as if beckoning him to come closer.

"Finn, my boy... come home."

"Finn, don't!" Isadora's voice cut through the haze, bringing him back to reality. The figure vanished, leaving only the mist and the silence. He shook his head, his mind clearing, and he felt Isadora's hand on his arm, grounding him.

"Thank you," he murmured, his voice shaky. "I don't know what came over me."

She gave him a worried look. "This forest is trying to lure us away. It's testing us, drawing out our deepest desires and fears. Stay strong."

They pressed on, but the whispers grew louder, more insistent, calling to each of them. Finn saw Cedric's face tighten as he glanced around, his gaze haunted, as if he were seeing ghosts from his past. Roderic's eyes darted from side to side, his usually confident expression faltering, as though he were being pulled in different directions.

Then, without warning, a figure appeared before them—a young woman with dark hair and a sad, gentle smile, reaching out a hand to Roderic. He stopped, his eyes widening.

"Amara?" he whispered, his voice filled with shock and longing.

The woman's smile widened, and she stepped closer, her voice soft and sorrowful. "Roderic, it's me. I'm here. Come with me."

Finn grabbed Roderic's arm, pulling him back. "It's not real, Roderic. She's not real."

Roderic shook his head, as if waking from a dream, but his gaze lingered on the fading image. "I—I thought I'd lost her," he murmured, his voice thick with emotion. "She... she was my family, once."

Finn gave his friend a reassuring squeeze. "This place is using our memories against us. It wants to separate us. We can't let it."

But the forest was relentless, surrounding them with whispers and shadows, each vision more tempting than the last. As they moved deeper, Finn felt an ache in his heart, a growing pull to turn back, to leave the mission behind and seek peace. The voices offered promises of rest, of safety, of home, each one more alluring than the last.

They came to a fork in the path, the mist swirling around them, obscuring the way forward. The trees seemed to shift, creating multiple paths that led in different directions, each one shrouded in mystery. Finn could feel the forest pushing them apart, each path seeming to call to one of them, inviting them to walk alone.

Cedric glanced at each path, his face hardening with resolve. "We stay together. No matter what we see or hear, we do not separate."

But the voices grew louder, echoing in their minds, each one designed to weaken their resolve, to make them doubt. The forest was alive, tugging at their loyalties, testing the strength of their bond.

A figure appeared on one of the paths, an elderly man with a face lined with wisdom and sorrow, his voice filled with pain as he looked at Cedric. "You abandoned us, Cedric. You left us in our darkest hour. How can you lead them now?"

Cedric's face hardened, his hands clenching into fists. He shook his head, taking a step back. "No. I chose to protect what I could. I can't let you haunt me now."

The figure faded, but Finn could see the pain in Cedric's eyes, the memories of decisions he could never undo.

Then Isadora gasped, and Finn turned to see a vision standing before her—a group of people, cloaked in the robes of mages, their faces stern and unforgiving.

"Isadora," one of them said, his voice cold. "You were never strong enough. You never belonged with us. Why do you think you can succeed now?"

Tears welled up in Isadora's eyes, but she lifted her chin, facing the illusion with quiet strength. "You may think that, but my strength doesn't come from you. It comes from within, and from my friends."

The figures vanished, leaving only the mist, but Finn could see the shadow of doubt still lingering in her eyes.

And then it was Finn's turn. A figure appeared before him, someone he didn't expect—himself. A version of himself that looked older, worn down by the weight of the crown, his face lined with sorrow and regret.

"Do you really think you're worthy of this, Finn?" his own voice whispered, dripping with self-doubt. "You're just a squire. What makes you think you can lead them, let alone save an entire kingdom?"

Finn's heart pounded, the doubts rising like a dark wave within him. But he remembered his friends' voices, their belief in him, the sacrifices they had made to be here. He took a steadying breath and forced himself to meet his own gaze.

"I may not have all the answers," he whispered, his voice filled with determination. "But I have courage, and I have those who believe in me. That's enough."

The vision faded, and the mist began to recede, the oppressive weight of the forest lifting as their resolve held strong. One by one, the illusions vanished, leaving only the silent, shadowed woods around them. They had faced their doubts, confronted their fears, and held on to the truth of their loyalty to each other.

Cedric looked around, relief in his eyes. "We made it through. The forest tried to tear us apart, but it failed."

Roderic managed a small, shaky smile. "Well, that was… unpleasant. I don't think I'll be revisiting any of those memories anytime soon."

Isadora nodded, her expression thoughtful but resolute. "The forest tried to break us, but it only made us stronger. Whatever lies ahead, we know now that we can face it together."

Finn felt a surge of pride and gratitude for his friends. They had survived the Whispering Woods, each of them tested by the voices of their past, yet they had held onto their loyalty, their bond stronger than ever. As they continued through the forest, he knew that they would face more trials, each one more challenging than the last. But he also knew that as long as they stayed together, no magic, no curse, could break them.

They emerged from the woods at last, the final whispers fading into silence. The path ahead was clear, the air fresher, as though the forest itself had acknowledged their strength and released them.

With the strength of their bond renewed and their spirits unbroken, Finn led his companions onward, toward whatever trials lay ahead, knowing that together, they could face anything.

Chapter 19: A Tale of Betrayal

The path out of the Whispering Woods led Finn and his companions to a narrow, rocky trail carved along the edge of a sheer cliff. Below, waves crashed against jagged rocks, sending sprays of white foam into the air. The wind whipped around them, sharp and biting, adding to the tension that had grown heavy between them since the forest. Each of them seemed lost in their own thoughts, the whispers of the woods still haunting them, lingering doubts hanging in the air like a storm waiting to break.

They had survived the trials of the Whispering Woods, yet a strange feeling gnawed at Finn, a sense that something was amiss. The memory of the Bandit Queen's words echoed in his mind: "Remember, there will come a time when you must choose again. And the next choice may not be as forgiving."

He shook off the feeling, focusing on the path ahead, but as they approached a narrow stretch along the cliffside, Roderic, who had been walking at the back of the group, suddenly halted.

"Roderic, what is it?" Finn asked, glancing back.

Roderic's face was tense, his expression unreadable as he stepped forward, his hand hovering over the dagger at his side. His eyes darted to Finn, then to the others, and finally settled on the path ahead, as if he were weighing his options.

"I think... I think we need to talk, Finn," Roderic said, his tone strained. "Before we go any further."

Finn felt a prickle of unease. "What's going on, Roderic?"

Roderic's face hardened, his jaw clenched. "Look, this whole quest, this crown... it's all a fool's errand. We're risking our lives for a relic that will only curse the next king and drain him dry. I didn't sign up to throw my life away for a kingdom that doesn't even know my name."

Isadora stepped forward, her eyes narrowing. "We all knew the risks, Roderic. You agreed to this mission because you believed in it."

Roderic scoffed, his gaze darkening. "Believed in it? I joined because I was promised something. Gold, freedom, a chance to start over. Not this—this endless nightmare of sacrifices and curses. And now I'm done."

Cedric's face tightened, his voice low and dangerous. "Are you saying you're abandoning us?"

"Not exactly," Roderic replied, a strange glint in his eye. He drew his dagger, pointing it at Finn. "The way I see it, I can still come out of this alive... if I play my cards right. I made a deal before we left. If I bring you back—or at least the map and the clues we've gathered—I walk away rich."

Finn's heart sank, realization dawning on him. "You... you made a deal to betray us?"

Roderic's gaze flickered with something like regret, but it was fleeting. "Look, Finn, you don't understand. I don't have the kind of loyalty you all do. I've survived by looking out for myself, not by playing the hero. If you hand over the map and the clues, I'll let you go. But if you won't... then this ends here."

Isadora gasped, stepping back in shock. "Roderic, don't do this. We're friends."

Roderic's face twisted in frustration. "Friends? You don't know the first thing about me. I'm just a thief to you, a tool to use and then discard once we're done."

Finn's anger flared, but he forced himself to stay calm. "That's not true, Roderic. You've been a part of this team, a part of this journey. You've helped us through every trial. You don't have to do this."

Roderic shook his head, his expression torn. "I don't want to, Finn, but... but I don't see another way. I can't go back empty-handed, and I can't keep pretending I belong here. So give me the map. Now."

Finn's gaze hardened, and he drew his sword, his stance steady. "I can't do that, Roderic. Not after everything we've been through. We're too close to give up now."

Roderic's face twisted in anger and desperation. "Then you leave me no choice."

Without warning, he lunged at Finn, his dagger flashing in the dim light. Finn barely had time to parry the strike, his sword clashing against Roderic's dagger with a sharp ring. The narrow cliffside path left little room for manoeuvring, forcing them into a deadly dance along the edge.

Cedric and Isadora stood frozen, their faces stricken with disbelief, but Finn's focus remained on Roderic, each of them struggling for an advantage. The wind howled around them, and the rocks beneath their feet shifted, adding a treacherous element to the fight.

"Roderic, stop!" Finn shouted, blocking another vicious strike. "You don't have to do this!"

But Roderic's expression was wild, as though he were beyond reason, driven by fear and desperation. "It's too late, Finn. I don't belong in your world, and I never did!"

He lunged again, forcing Finn back toward the cliff's edge. Finn's foot slipped on a loose stone, and he felt himself sway dangerously close to the edge, his heart pounding as he fought to regain his balance.

In that moment, Cedric rushed forward, his sword drawn. "Enough, Roderic. Stand down, before you do something you can't undo."

But Roderic only snarled, twisting to face Cedric. "You don't understand, old man. This is survival. Something you'd never understand, with all your noble honour and loyalty."

Roderic struck at Cedric, but Cedric blocked him, his face a mask of sorrow and determination. "Survival isn't betrayal. Survival is trusting the people by your side, the people who've risked everything for you."

Roderic hesitated, his dagger wavering, but then he shook his head, his face a mix of anger and regret. "I'm sorry, but I can't. I can't trust anyone."

He turned back to Finn, his dagger raised for one final strike, but Finn saw an opening. Summoning all his strength, he lunged forward, knocking the dagger from Roderic's hand and pinning him against the rocky wall.

"Roderic," Finn said, his voice steady but filled with sorrow. "We trusted you. I trusted you. Why couldn't you trust us?"

Roderic looked away, his face filled with shame and bitterness. "I don't know, Finn. I... I don't know how."

For a moment, there was only the sound of the wind and the distant crash of waves below. Finn released his grip, stepping back, his heart heavy. Roderic slumped against the wall, his face twisted with regret and anger, as though he hated himself as much as he hated his choice.

Isadora stepped forward, her voice soft. "We would have helped you, Roderic. You didn't have to do this alone."

Roderic shook his head, his voice barely more than a whisper. "Maybe... maybe I just never learned how to believe in anyone."

Cedric sheathed his sword, his gaze sorrowful. "There's always a choice, Roderic. Even now."

Roderic let out a bitter laugh. "Maybe for you, there is. But for people like me... trust doesn't come so easily." He looked at Finn, a flicker of something softer in his eyes. "You're a good leader, Finn. Better than I deserved."

Before any of them could respond, Roderic turned and began walking down the path, his figure disappearing into the mist. They watched him go, a mixture of anger, sadness, and disappointment in their hearts.

Finn's hands trembled as he sheathed his sword, his mind reeling from the confrontation. He had trusted Roderic, considered him a friend, and the betrayal stung more deeply than he had expected. But as he looked at Cedric and Isadora, he felt a renewed sense of determination.

Isadora placed a hand on his shoulder, her eyes filled with sympathy. "We've lost him, but we're still here, Finn. And we'll see this through to the end, no matter what."

Cedric nodded, his gaze unwavering. "This mission means more than any one person's mistakes. We carry on, for the kingdom, and for each other."

Finn nodded, swallowing back the bitterness that lingered in his heart. The path ahead was more dangerous than ever, but he knew he could rely on Cedric and Isadora. They were bound by a loyalty Roderic could never understand.

With his allies by his side, Finn turned toward the path ahead, ready to face whatever lay beyond the cliffs, his heart hardened and his resolve stronger than ever.

Chapter 20: The Hidden Waterfall

The air was thick with mist as Finn, Cedric, and Isadora followed the sound of rushing water echoing through the forest. After the painful events on the cliffside, they had travelled in silence, each lost in their own thoughts. But the journey had to continue, and Finn knew that the next clue was close. They could hear the waterfall before they saw it, its powerful roar growing louder with each step.

Finally, they reached a small clearing, where the forest opened up to reveal a magnificent waterfall cascading over a rocky cliff into a serene pool below. Sunlight filtered through the trees, casting rainbows in the mist, giving the place an ethereal beauty that seemed to hold a promise. Finn felt a sense of anticipation building within him as he scanned the area, searching for something that might lead them closer to the crown.

Cedric approached the edge of the pool, his eyes narrowing as he studied the waterfall. "This is no ordinary waterfall," he murmured. "Look at the way the rock juts out at the base—it's as though it's hiding something."

Finn nodded, stepping closer. "There must be something behind it. The clues have led us here for a reason."

Isadora joined them, her face thoughtful. "If there's an inscription or another clue, it could be hidden behind the water. We'll have to go through it."

With a determined look, Finn led the way, stepping into the cold spray of the waterfall. The water pounded down, drenching them instantly, but they pushed through, moving along the slippery stones at the edge of the pool. As they reached the base of the waterfall, Finn could just make out the faint shape of an opening behind the curtain of water.

He gestured to the others, and they carefully made their way into the hidden alcove. Inside, the roar of the waterfall was muted, replaced by a hushed stillness that felt almost sacred. The space was dimly lit, with water dripping from the ceiling, and at the far end, etched into the rock, was an ancient inscription carved in elegant, flowing script.

Isadora stepped forward, running her fingers over the worn symbols. "This language... it's old, very old. But I think I can translate it."

She took a deep breath, tracing each word carefully as she read aloud:

"In the land where shadows and light entwine,
Lies the place of the hidden sign.
Three paths converge where rivers meet,
And only the worthy shall claim the seat.
Beyond the veil of emerald green,
Where truth is found but rarely seen.
Seek not with sight, but with the heart,
And there the final journey shall start."

The words seemed to hang in the air, filling the alcove with a sense of mystery and gravity. Finn felt a shiver run down his spine. Each line of the riddle was like a piece of the puzzle they had been putting together since the beginning, hinting at the crown's location but concealing it behind layers of meaning.

Cedric crossed his arms, his brow furrowed in thought. "Where shadows and light entwine... it sounds like a place that's both hidden and accessible, somewhere on the border of light and dark."

Isadora nodded. "And 'three paths converge where rivers meet.' That must be a specific location—a place where three rivers come together. It would have to be a significant landmark."

Finn considered the other lines, his mind racing. "Beyond the veil of emerald green..." The phrase seemed to imply something natural, like a forest or grove, and the idea of seeking with the heart rather than sight suggested that the crown could not simply be found through ordinary means.

He looked at Cedric and Isadora, his face set with determination. "It sounds like the place we're looking for is a sacred spot—a place where nature and magic meet. Somewhere hidden, yet known to those who understand the land's power."

Cedric nodded, his eyes brightening with realization. "I believe I know of a place that fits. It's called the Valley of Verdant Shadows, an ancient forest where three rivers converge. It's said to be a place of deep magic, where the old ways are still honoured. Few dare enter, and even fewer return."

Isadora's gaze sharpened. "That has to be it. The valley would be 'beyond the veil of emerald green,' and if it's as magical as the stories say, it could easily be a place where illusions hide the truth."

Finn felt a surge of hope. They were close, closer than they had ever been, and despite the hardships they had endured, despite Roderic's betrayal, they had found the next piece of the puzzle.

But as they turned to leave the alcove, a low rumble echoed through the cave, and the ground trembled beneath their feet. Finn's heart skipped a beat as rocks began to fall from the ceiling, the narrow space shuddering as if the mountain itself were trying to expel them.

"Move!" Cedric shouted, pushing Finn and Isadora toward the entrance.

They scrambled through the cascade of water, dodging falling stones and slipping on the wet rocks. Just as they emerged from behind the waterfall, the alcove collapsed entirely, sealing the ancient inscription and leaving only the cascading water where it had been.

Breathless, they moved back to the clearing, their hearts pounding. Cedric scanned the area, ensuring they were safe, and then looked at Finn with a grim smile. "It seems that even the land itself tests our resolve."

Finn let out a shaky laugh, his adrenaline still pumping. "Maybe it does. But at least we have our answer."

Isadora brushed the water from her face, her expression serious. "The Valley of Verdant Shadows is no ordinary place. If the crown is there, it won't be unguarded. We'll need to be prepared for anything."

They gathered their belongings, their resolve renewed. The journey to the Valley of Verdant Shadows would not be easy, but Finn felt a new sense of purpose as they set off. They were closer than ever to finding the crown, and though the path ahead was fraught with danger, he knew that he could trust his remaining allies. The trials they had faced had tested their loyalty and their courage, and now, with the valley's location in mind, he felt that the final test awaited them.

As they walked away from the waterfall, Finn cast one last glance over his shoulder, a sense of awe and reverence filling him. The crown was near, hidden in the heart of a place where magic and nature met. And he knew, with every step he took, that he was ready to face whatever final trials lay ahead.

Chapter 21: Captured by the Enemy

The path to the Valley of Verdant Shadows was long and treacherous, winding through dense forests and rugged terrain. Finn, Cedric, and Isadora pressed on, their spirits lifted by the knowledge that they were close to finding the crown. But as they entered a narrow canyon, an eerie silence fell, and Finn's instincts prickled with a sense of danger.

Suddenly, shadows moved among the rocks above them, and before Finn could react, a group of heavily armed soldiers descended, blocking their path. Each soldier bore a crest that Finn recognized instantly—the crest of the king's most feared rival, Lord Morgath, a ruthless noble who sought to overthrow the kingdom and seize power for himself.

"Run!" Cedric shouted, drawing his sword. He and Isadora barely had time to prepare before the soldiers swarmed around them, overwhelming them with sheer numbers. Finn fought back as best as he could, but within moments, he was struck from behind. The world went black.

When Finn came to, he was bound and blindfolded, his head throbbing from the blow. He could hear the sounds of clinking metal and murmuring voices, a low and ominous hum that filled the air with dread. They had been captured by Morgath's forces, the very enemies who would stop at nothing to keep the crown hidden, to keep Eldoria under their control.

The blindfold was yanked off, and Finn blinked, his vision adjusting to the dim light of the tent he was in. Lord Morgath stood before him, a tall, cold figure with sharp features and eyes that gleamed with cruel intelligence. His armour was black and silver, adorned with symbols of power, and his smile was one of pure malice.

"So, the king's squire," Morgath sneered, his voice smooth and mocking. "The boy who thinks he can save the kingdom by chasing old legends. How amusing."

Finn glared at him, refusing to show fear. "The people of Eldoria won't follow you, Morgath. They know what you are—a tyrant who only wants power."

Morgath laughed, a sound devoid of warmth. "You think the people care who sits on the throne? They care only for survival, and I offer them stability. Unlike your feeble king, who hides behind relics and fairy tales."

He stepped closer, his gaze turning cold. "I know you seek the crown, boy. Tell me where it is, and perhaps I'll show you mercy."

Finn remained silent, meeting Morgath's gaze defiantly. He would never reveal the location of the crown, even if it meant enduring whatever Morgath had planned.

Morgath's face darkened, and he nodded to one of his men. "Very well. Let's see if a little persuasion will loosen your tongue."

The soldiers seized Finn, dragging him to a post in the center of the tent and binding him tightly. They struck him across the face, then again, each blow harder than the last. Pain shot through him, but he bit down, refusing to cry out. His mind drifted to his friends, hoping they had managed to escape. He could endure this if it meant keeping the crown's location safe, if it meant protecting Cedric and Isadora.

The torture continued, each question from Morgath met with silence. Finn's vision blurred, pain consuming him, but still he refused to speak. His mind clung to memories of the journey so far, the sacrifices his friends had made, the loyalty that had carried him through every trial. He couldn't betray that.

Just when he felt his strength slipping, he heard a commotion outside the tent. Shouts, the clash of metal, and then the tent flap was thrown open. Through the haze of pain, he saw a familiar figure—a tall, lean man with quick movements and a dagger in each hand.

It was Roderic.

Finn blinked, barely able to process what he was seeing. Roderic moved with deadly efficiency, taking down two guards with swift

THE LOST KING'S CROWN

strikes. He grabbed one of the soldiers by the collar, shoving him aside, and then rushed toward Finn, his face tense with urgency.

"Come on, squire," Roderic muttered, cutting through the ropes binding Finn. "I didn't come all this way to watch you get yourself killed."

Finn could barely stand, but Roderic looped an arm around him, supporting his weight. "Roderic... why?" he managed to choke out, disbelief mixing with gratitude.

Roderic gave a small, grim smile. "Let's just say I had a change of heart. Now shut up and move, or we'll both end up in Morgath's dungeon."

With Roderic's help, Finn stumbled out of the tent and into the chaos outside. Roderic had somehow managed to create a diversion, setting fire to some of the tents and scattering Morgath's soldiers. They wove through the confusion, slipping into the shadows as they made their way out of the camp.

As they reached the edge of the forest, Roderic paused, catching his breath. He looked at Finn, his expression serious. "I didn't expect to come back," he admitted, his voice low. "But... seeing you all fight, seeing you risk everything for a kingdom that's barely given you anything—it made me realize something."

Finn watched him, still stunned, waiting for him to continue.

Roderic glanced away, his face shadowed with guilt. "I've spent my life looking out for myself, surviving however I could. I thought I could live with that, but when I walked away... it didn't feel right. You trusted me, and I betrayed that trust. I'm not asking for forgiveness, but I can at least make things right."

A rush of emotion welled up in Finn's chest, and despite everything, he managed a small, pained smile. "Roderic... thank you."

Roderic sighed, a hint of his old smirk returning. "Don't get all mushy on me, squire. I'm not exactly a hero yet."

At that moment, they heard footsteps approaching, and Finn's heart leapt as he saw Cedric and Isadora hurrying toward them, relief evident on their faces.

"Finn!" Isadora cried, rushing to his side. "We thought we'd lost you."

Cedric clasped Roderic's shoulder, his face a mixture of respect and approval. "You came back for him. I didn't think you had it in you."

Roderic shrugged, a faint grin tugging at his lips. "Neither did I."

With Finn leaning on Cedric for support, the group made their way deeper into the forest, putting as much distance as possible between themselves and Morgath's camp. Once they found a safe spot, they settled down, giving Finn a chance to rest and recover from his injuries.

As they sat around a small, hidden campfire, Roderic finally broke the silence. "Look, I know I messed up. I betrayed you, and I won't pretend it's easy to forgive. But if you'll let me, I'd like to see this through. I don't want to be the kind of man who runs when things get hard. Not anymore."

Finn looked at him, the pain of the betrayal still fresh, but something in Roderic's face told him that he was sincere. The journey had changed all of them, brought out parts of themselves they hadn't known were there. And maybe, just maybe, there was a chance for redemption.

"You're welcome to stay with us, Roderic," Finn said quietly. "As long as you're here for the right reasons."

Roderic nodded, his face sombre. "I am."

With that, they sat in silence, the fire crackling softly, each of them lost in their thoughts. The journey ahead would be no easier, and Morgath would not give up the pursuit. But for now, Finn felt a renewed sense of hope. They were battered, bruised, but together—and together, they would see this quest to its end.

They had faced betrayal, pain, and fear, yet each trial had only strengthened their bond. With Roderic's return, Finn knew they had gained not just an ally, but a friend who had finally found his place, standing by their side in the fight to save Eldoria.

Chapter 22: The Underground Labyrinth

The entrance to the labyrinth was hidden beneath a dense grove of trees, concealed by moss and shadows. Only a faint marking—a spiral etched into a stone slab—gave any hint of what lay beneath. Finn, Cedric, Isadora, and Roderic gathered around the entrance, each feeling a mix of apprehension and determination. This labyrinth was rumoured to be one of the final obstacles guarding the crown's resting place, a maze of darkness and silence that had claimed the minds of those unprepared for its trials.

"This is it," Cedric said, his voice steady but grim. "The Labyrinth of Shadows. Few who enter ever find their way back."

Finn took a deep breath, feeling the weight of the mission settle on his shoulders. "We're not turning back now. Whatever we face in there, we face it together."

Roderic smirked, though his face held a trace of worry. "A little late to back out, isn't it? Besides, I'm too stubborn to let some shadows and whispers stop me."

Isadora nodded, though she looked sombre. "The labyrinth will likely test each of us in ways we can't anticipate. We'll need to trust ourselves—and each other."

With one last look at each other, they descended into the labyrinth. The passage was steep and narrow, winding downward in a series of rough stone steps that grew darker with each step. Soon, the light from the entrance faded, leaving only the faint glow of Isadora's magic, which flickered around her fingertips like a beacon.

As they ventured deeper, the oppressive silence settled around them, pressing in like a physical force. The air grew colder, and a faint, stale odour permeated the darkness. They could hear nothing but their own footsteps echoing through the narrow corridors, and each sound seemed to amplify, creating an eerie, disorienting effect.

After what felt like hours of walking, they reached a large chamber with three separate paths leading in different directions. Each path seemed identical, disappearing into the pitch-blackness, giving no indication of what lay beyond.

"We choose one and hope for the best," Cedric said, studying each passage.

But before they could decide, the ground trembled, and a stone wall slid into place behind them, sealing off the chamber from the way they had come. An ominous rumble echoed through the chamber, and the torchlight flickered, casting eerie shadows that danced along the walls.

Then, without warning, the torches extinguished, plunging them into complete darkness.

"Stay close!" Finn shouted, reaching out, but as he did, he felt nothing but empty air. His heart pounded as he called out again, "Cedric? Isadora? Roderic?"

Only silence answered him.

Finn realized, with a sinking feeling, that he was alone. The labyrinth had separated them.

The darkness pressed in on him, thick and suffocating, and the silence was so profound that he could hear his own heartbeat echoing in his ears. Panic clawed at him, but he forced himself to take deep breaths, to remember that he wasn't truly alone. His friends were somewhere in the labyrinth, likely facing their own trials.

Stay calm, he told himself, focusing on the words of the druid's prophecy. Seek not with sight, but with the heart.

He reached out, feeling along the cold stone wall, and began to walk forward, his hands his only guide. The darkness was absolute, disorienting, and as he moved, he began to feel a strange sense of isolation, as if he were drifting further and further away from everything he knew.

Meanwhile, in another part of the labyrinth, Isadora found herself in a narrow corridor that stretched endlessly in both directions. The silence was unsettling, an unnatural stillness that seemed to amplify every thought and doubt in her mind. She tried calling out, but her voice felt muffled, as though swallowed by the walls themselves. She pressed forward, but each step felt heavier, her fears whispering that she might be trapped here forever, lost in this place of silence and shadows.

Roderic, too, was alone, but his surroundings were different—a series of narrow passages twisting and turning like the coils of a snake. He moved quickly, keeping a hand on the wall to guide him, but the darkness seemed to warp around him, playing tricks on his mind. Shadows flickered just out of reach, and he could swear he heard footsteps behind him, though he knew he was alone.

Cedric, meanwhile, found himself in a chamber where faint light flickered, illuminating a row of mirrors on each side of the walls. He caught his reflection in the mirrors, but as he walked, he noticed that the reflections were wrong—warped, twisted versions of himself that stared back with accusing eyes. He tried to ignore them, to move forward, but the reflections whispered his failures, his regrets, each one magnifying the guilt he carried.

As each of them walked through their individual paths, the labyrinth continued to play on their deepest fears, dredging up memories and doubts that tested their will. Yet, through the darkness and the silence, one thought persisted in each of their minds—the memory of their friends, the bond they shared, the loyalty that had brought them this far.

Finn stumbled through the darkness, feeling exhaustion set in, his mind beginning to fray. But then he remembered Cedric's voice, steady and calm, reminding him to hold onto his strength. He remembered Isadora's gentle words of encouragement and Roderic's dry humour, each memory like a small flame in the darkness. Slowly, he felt his resolve returning.

THE LOST KING'S CROWN

In another part of the labyrinth, Isadora closed her eyes, focusing on her magic, allowing the faint glow from her fingertips to light her way. She thought of Finn's determination, of Cedric's quiet strength, and Roderic's surprising loyalty, each thought grounding her, reminding her that she was not truly alone.

Roderic, too, found himself holding onto memories of the journey, of the times his friends had saved him, the loyalty they had shown despite his flaws. He clenched his fists, pushing forward, refusing to let the shadows break him.

And Cedric, standing before the twisted reflections, remembered the trust Finn had placed in him, the hope that each of them carried. He straightened, his gaze hardening, and turned away from the mirrors, finding his own path through the maze.

One by one, they overcame their fears, pushing forward through the labyrinth. And as each of them took a step in their respective passages, a faint light appeared at the end of the corridor, guiding them back toward the center.

Eventually, they emerged into a large chamber where four paths converged, reuniting them at last. Relief flooded through each of them as they saw each other, exhaustion mingling with gratitude.

"Is everyone alright?" Finn asked, his voice hoarse but filled with relief.

Cedric nodded, his face lined with weariness. "We made it through, though it wasn't easy."

Isadora's eyes shone with quiet pride. "The labyrinth tried to break us, to isolate us, but it failed. Our bond is stronger than its illusions."

Roderic managed a faint smirk, though there was genuine relief in his expression. "Well, that was suitably horrifying. But I'd rather be here with all of you than alone in there."

In the center of the chamber, they saw a small pedestal, and atop it lay a worn scroll, bound with a ribbon and covered in dust. Finn reached forward, untying the ribbon and unfurling the scroll, revealing another riddle:

"When the light and shadows both align,
Follow the path where stars shall shine.
In the Valley of Verdant Shadows deep,
Where the roots of power sleep."

The words filled him with hope, each line pointing them toward their final destination—the Valley of Verdant Shadows, the place where the crown of Eldoria awaited them.

Finn looked at his friends, a renewed sense of determination in his heart. "This is it. The crown is within reach, just beyond the valley. We've come this far, and we're ready for whatever lies ahead."

With a final glance around the labyrinth, they made their way toward the exit, each of them carrying the scars and strength of their trials. They had faced darkness, silence, and isolation, but they had emerged stronger, their loyalty unshaken.

Together, they climbed out of the depths of the labyrinth, ready to face the final challenge. The crown was close, the fate of Eldoria within their grasp—and with their bond unbroken, they knew they could overcome any trial that awaited them in the Valley of Verdant Shadows.

Chapter 23: The Broken Mirror

As Finn and his companions left the labyrinth, they found themselves in a narrow clearing, surrounded by towering trees whose branches intertwined overhead, casting a thick canopy that blocked out most of the light. In the center of the clearing stood an ornate mirror, framed in twisted vines and encrusted with gleaming stones that shimmered even in the dim light. It looked ancient, but its glass was perfectly clear, giving off a soft, eerie glow that seemed to draw them in.

Finn approached the mirror cautiously, feeling an unsettling pull, as though the mirror itself were watching them. He remembered the druid's warning about tests that would challenge not only their courage but their hearts and minds as well.

"What do you think it is?" Isadora asked, her voice barely above a whisper, as though afraid to disturb the silence.

Cedric's face was tense as he studied the mirror. "I've heard of magical mirrors used to test the strength of those who look into them. They show visions... reflections of possibilities, some say of the future."

Roderic scoffed, though there was unease in his eyes. "Great. Just what we need—more disturbing visions."

Finn took a deep breath, steeling himself. "We're close to the end, closer than ever before. If this mirror is here, it's meant to test us, to make us question everything we've fought for."

Isadora nodded. "Whatever it shows, we face it together."

One by one, they stepped in front of the mirror, each of them seeing different visions play out in the glass. And as they watched, each vision grew darker, more horrifying, showing a future that could come to pass if they failed in their mission.

Finn's Vision

As Finn looked into the mirror, the glass began to swirl with mist, and an image formed—a scene of Eldoria shrouded in darkness. The kingdom lay in ruins, its fields barren, its towns empty. Shadows moved across the landscape, consuming everything in their path, and in the distance, the castle stood in decay, its walls crumbling, its towers broken.

Finn saw himself standing alone in the ruins of the kingdom, older, wearier, with deep lines etched into his face. He looked defeated, his shoulders slumped, his gaze hollow. He was clad in tattered armour, his sword rusted and broken at his side. The weight of failure hung over him, and as he looked closer, he saw that the land itself had withered, its magic faded.

A voice echoed from the depths of the mirror, cold and mocking: "You could have saved them, but you were not strong enough. You did not have the courage to see it through."

The vision filled Finn with a sense of despair so deep it felt as though he were drowning in it. This was the future that awaited Eldoria if he failed, if he let fear or doubt hold him back. But as the image faded, he felt a spark ignite within him—a fierce resolve, a refusal to let this dark future come to pass.

Isadora's Vision

When Isadora stepped in front of the mirror, she saw herself standing in a ruined library, the walls scorched and crumbling, shelves of ancient books reduced to ashes. She reached out, her fingers trembling as she touched the charred remains of what had once been her sanctuary, her source of knowledge.

In the vision, she saw herself alone, her magical light dim and fading. Her powers, which had once been strong and vibrant, now flickered weakly, like a candle struggling to stay lit. The spells she tried to cast fizzled and failed, and she saw fear in her own eyes, a desperation she had never known before.

A voice whispered through the mirror, cold and biting: "You were never strong enough. Your magic was always a flickering light, easily extinguished. You have failed those who depended on you."

Isadora's heart ached as she watched the vision, the weight of failure pressing down on her. But deep within, she felt her determination solidify, a fierce will to prove that she was stronger than her fears. She would not let this future come to pass; she would wield her magic to protect those she loved.

Cedric's Vision

Cedric stepped up to the mirror, his jaw set, but as he gazed into the glass, his face paled. He saw himself alone in a vast, desolate battlefield, surrounded by the remnants of fallen soldiers, their faces twisted in agony. He knelt among them, his sword lying uselessly at his side, his armour tarnished and broken.

In the vision, he looked weary, older, as though he had fought endless battles but achieved nothing. The weight of loss was etched into his face, and he seemed haunted by the ghosts of those he had failed to protect. He could hear their voices, accusing him, their cries filling the air with sorrow.

A voice spoke from the mirror, low and mournful: "You could have saved them, but your strength was not enough. You abandoned them to their fate."

Cedric's heart clenched at the vision, the faces of his fallen comrades searing into his mind. But as the image faded, he felt a surge of defiance. He had vowed to protect those he loved, to stand by Finn and Isadora. This vision would not come true—he would not fail them.

Roderic's Vision

When Roderic looked into the mirror, he saw himself in a dark, empty alley, surrounded by shadows. He was alone, his face etched with regret, his eyes hollow and haunted. His once-quick hands were now slow, trembling, his daggers dull and rusted. He had spent his life running, surviving by any means necessary, but now he looked lost, defeated.

In the vision, he heard the voices of his friends calling out to him, but he could not reach them. He was trapped in his solitude, consumed by the guilt of betrayal, his past mistakes echoing in his mind, haunting him endlessly.

A voice hissed through the mirror, cold and accusing: "You abandoned those who trusted you, left them to face darkness alone. You are nothing but a shadow, forever alone."

Roderic's throat tightened, his heart pounding with the weight of the vision. But as the mirror's image faded, he clenched his fists, his face set with determination. He would not become this broken man. He would prove his loyalty, earn his place by their side, and ensure that they would not face darkness alone.

When each of them stepped back from the mirror, there was a heavy silence. Each of them had glimpsed a future they could not accept—a world where they failed, where the kingdom suffered because they had been unable to see their mission through. The mirror had shown them the darkest possible outcome, and though the visions lingered in their minds, filling them with dread, they felt a renewed determination burning within them.

Finn looked at his friends, their faces pale but resolute. "We won't let that happen," he said, his voice steady. "Those futures... they're only possible if we give up, if we let fear control us."

Isadora nodded, her face set with fierce resolve. "The mirror showed us what could happen, but it doesn't have to. We have the power to change it."

Cedric placed a hand on Finn's shoulder, his gaze unwavering. "We face these fears, not as individuals, but as a team. Together, we're stronger than any darkness that lies ahead."

Roderic managed a small smile, his usual bravado tempered by sincerity. "If those visions are supposed to scare us off, they'll have to try harder. We've come too far to back down now."

With newfound resolve, they turned away from the mirror, leaving its dark visions behind. The path ahead led into the Valley of Verdant Shadows, where the crown awaited, hidden in a place where magic and nature converged. The mirror had tested their courage, revealing their deepest fears, but they had emerged stronger, their bond unbroken.

They moved forward, their steps in sync, each of them carrying the weight of their vision yet determined to change the course of their destiny. Whatever challenges awaited them in the Valley of Verdant Shadows, they would face them together, united by their shared resolve and strengthened by the knowledge that they had the power to create a brighter future for Eldoria.

Chapter 24: The Curse of the Crown

The Valley of Verdant Shadows was unlike any place Finn and his companions had encountered. Ancient trees towered above them, their leaves casting a deep, green glow that seemed almost supernatural. The air was thick with magic, humming with an energy that made the hair on Finn's arms stand on end. This was the place where the crown had been hidden—where the magic of Eldoria was strongest.

At the heart of the valley, they found an ancient stone altar, covered in vines and moss, with carvings that depicted the history of Eldoria. Atop the altar sat a small, ornate chest, locked and bound with enchanted chains. Finn approached it slowly, feeling both awe and a strange sense of dread. This was it. The crown of Eldoria.

But as he reached out, Isadora placed a hand on his arm, her face troubled. "Wait, Finn. There's something... something strange here."

Cedric moved closer, his brow furrowing as he examined the altar. "These carvings... they tell a story, one that we haven't been told before."

Isadora's eyes swept over the carvings, her fingers tracing the ancient symbols. The story unfolded in fragments, scenes that told of a time long ago, when the crown was first forged. A powerful mage-king had bound his life to the land, creating the crown to ensure the kingdom's prosperity and protection. But as she continued reading, her expression grew darker, her voice low and trembling as she interpreted the story.

"The crown is... it's not just a symbol of power. It's a vessel for the magic of Eldoria," she murmured, her voice filled with awe and dread. "The king who wears it is bound to the land, his life force tied to the magic that sustains the kingdom."

Finn looked at her, a sinking feeling forming in his stomach. "What does that mean, Isadora?"

She met his gaze, her face pale. "It means that whoever wears the crown becomes the kingdom's protector, yes—but at a terrible cost. The crown doesn't just give its power freely. It drains the life of the one who wears it, feeding on their vitality to fuel its magic. It's both a blessing and a curse. The king sacrifices himself for Eldoria, slowly fading, until there's nothing left of him but... shadows and memories."

Roderic let out a low whistle, his face twisted in horror. "So the king... he withers away, giving his life to keep the kingdom safe. That's... that's a death sentence."

Cedric's face was grim, his gaze fixed on the crown's chest. "It explains why so many kings have struggled under its weight. They weren't just ruling—they were offering themselves up as a sacrifice for the land."

Finn felt a chill run down his spine. This was a truth that had been hidden, a secret kept from all but the chosen few who bore the crown. He thought of the current king, of the toll he had seen weigh on him, and it all made sense now. The strength of Eldoria came at the cost of the king's life, his very essence.

He looked at his companions, seeing the weight of the revelation settle over them, the horror and sadness in their eyes.

Isadora's voice was filled with sorrow. "Every king... every ruler who has worn this crown has made that sacrifice willingly, knowing that they would slowly lose themselves to the land. It's a bond of loyalty, but also a curse. And now, if we restore the crown, we're asking someone else to take on that burden."

Finn clenched his fists, his heart pounding. The mission that had seemed so straightforward—find the crown, restore it to the king, and save Eldoria—now felt more complex, more tragic. Whoever wore this crown would not merely rule; they would give up everything for the kingdom, knowing that they would eventually fade into nothingness.

Roderic shook his head, his face filled with disbelief. "So we're just supposed to find someone willing to sacrifice themselves? Who would do that?"

Cedric's voice was steady but filled with a quiet resolve. "There are those who would. Those who understand that the good of the many sometimes outweighs the good of the one."

Finn's mind was racing. He had taken on this journey out of loyalty to the king, out of a desire to protect Eldoria. But he hadn't understood the true nature of the crown, the cost that it demanded. Could he, in good conscience, place that burden on someone else? Or would he have to consider the possibility that, perhaps, he might be the one to bear it?

Isadora looked at Finn, her gaze filled with concern. "Finn... you don't have to do this. There has to be another way."

But Finn shook his head, a fierce resolve settling over him. "If this is what's needed to save Eldoria, then we can't turn back. The kingdom depends on the crown's magic, even if it's a curse. The land is dying without it, and so are the people."

Roderic sighed, his face shadowed with conflict. "This whole thing is madness. We're asking someone to walk willingly into their own destruction."

"But we're also giving them a chance to save Eldoria," Cedric replied quietly. "To give the kingdom a future. That's a sacrifice few would make, but it's one that means something."

They stood in silence, the weight of the crown's curse hanging heavily between them. Finally, Finn reached out, his hand hovering over the chest.

"We'll take the crown back to the king," he said, his voice steady. "He'll know what to do. If he chooses to bear it, we'll honour his sacrifice. And if he can't... we'll find another way to save Eldoria."

With a deep breath, he opened the chest, and there, nestled within, was the crown of Eldoria. It was even more beautiful than he had imagined, crafted from silver and gold, adorned with gemstones that seemed to glow with a light of their own. But as he looked closer, he could feel the weight of its magic, a power that was both alluring and ominous, a reminder of the lives it had claimed.

He lifted the crown carefully, feeling its energy pulse through him, a sensation that was both exhilarating and terrifying. This was the heart of Eldoria's magic, the source of its strength and the secret of its sacrifice.

They wrapped the crown in cloth, reverently placing it in Finn's pack, and turned to leave the valley. The truth of the crown had changed them all, deepening their resolve yet burdening them with the knowledge of its curse.

As they made their way back through the valley, Roderic broke the silence, his voice low. "You know, Finn, you don't have to be the one to carry this. We're in this together, for better or worse."

Finn looked at him, grateful for the support. "Thank you, Roderic. But I've come this far because I believe in the kingdom. Whatever comes next, we'll face it together."

Isadora nodded, a glint of determination in her eyes. "We'll see this through to the end, no matter what it takes."

Cedric placed a reassuring hand on Finn's shoulder. "We're with you, Finn. The kingdom needs the crown, but it also needs leaders who understand what it means to sacrifice. We'll make sure that sacrifice isn't in vain."

With the crown's terrible secret now known, they left the Valley of Verdant Shadows, the path back to Eldoria stretching before them. They had faced darkness, silence, and even betrayal, but the curse of the crown was a test unlike any other. And yet, as they walked, Finn felt a fierce sense of purpose. The burden of the crown was heavy, but they would carry it together.

In his heart, he knew that whatever fate awaited them, they would face it with courage, loyalty, and the knowledge that some sacrifices were worth making. For Eldoria, for the people, and for the kingdom they had sworn to protect, they would see this journey to its end, even if it demanded more than any of them had ever expected.

Act 4: The Race Against Time

Chapter 25: The Witch's Final Test

The journey back to the kingdom was tense and silent, each member of the group lost in their thoughts, weighed down by the revelation of the crown's curse. But as they emerged from the Valley of Verdant Shadows, they found themselves in a familiar clearing—the very place where they had first met the witch who had set them on this journey.

The air grew thick with magic, and a faint mist rose from the ground. Then, from the shadows, the witch stepped forward, her face partially hidden by the hood of her cloak, her eyes gleaming with a knowing intensity.

"I see you've uncovered the truth of the crown," she said, her voice smooth and cryptic. "You understand now the weight of what you seek to restore. But before you continue, there is one final test."

Finn exchanged a look with his companions, his hand instinctively going to the pack where the crown was safely wrapped. He knew that the witch was not one to interfere without purpose; she had guided them to this point, but he sensed this would be the last time she would do so.

"What kind of test?" Finn asked, his voice steady, though he felt a tremor of anticipation.

The witch smiled, a sad, knowing smile. "The final test is a test of worthiness, Finn. It is one thing to seek power, another to be willing to sacrifice for it. But true worthiness comes when you are faced with a choice that demands not only courage, but true selflessness. I need to know—are you willing to accept the burden of the crown, even if it means losing everything you hold dear?"

She extended her hand, and in her palm appeared a small vial filled with a dark, shimmering liquid. "Drink this," she said, "and it will show you the consequences of your choice. Only then can you decide if you are truly ready to bear the weight of Eldoria's magic."

THE LOST KING'S CROWN

Finn took a steadying breath, reaching out to take the vial. He felt the eyes of his friends on him, their silent support lending him strength. As he uncorked the vial, he glanced at them one last time, seeing the worry and trust in their faces.

"You don't have to do this alone, Finn," Isadora said softly, her voice filled with concern.

Cedric nodded, his expression grave. "Whatever this test demands, know that we stand with you."

With a final nod to his friends, Finn lifted the vial to his lips and drank. The liquid was bitter, cold, and it sent a shiver down his spine. Instantly, his vision blurred, and the world around him shifted, fading away into darkness.

Finn found himself standing alone in the throne room of Eldoria's castle. It was quiet, almost hauntingly so, with only the faintest light filtering through the stained glass windows. He looked down and saw that he was wearing a heavy crown on his head, its weight pressing down on him like a burden he could barely endure.

He turned and saw a line of faces staring at him—Cedric, Isadora, Roderic, and even the king himself. But their expressions were cold, distant, as if they did not recognize him. He tried to speak, to reach out to them, but they remained motionless, their eyes filled with disappointment and accusation.

A figure stepped forward, an older man who bore a striking resemblance to the current king. His face was lined with sorrow, his eyes hollow, and Finn realized with a start that he was looking at an echo of a former king, someone who had borne the crown's curse before him.

"This is the path you have chosen," the ghostly king said, his voice filled with a haunting sadness. "The crown demands everything from those who bear it. In the end, you will become part of the land, forgotten by those you love, remembered only by the stones and the roots of Eldoria."

Finn's heart pounded, the weight of the crown seeming to grow heavier with each word. He looked down at his hands and saw that they were aging before his eyes, his skin withering, his strength draining, until he felt more a shadow than a man.

"No," he whispered, fighting the despair that rose within him. "I'm doing this for them—for Eldoria. I can't let this kingdom fall."

The former king shook his head, his gaze both sympathetic and condemning. "But at what cost, Finn? This choice will demand everything from you, even the memory of who you once were. Is that a sacrifice you are truly willing to make?"

The vision shifted again, and Finn found himself in the midst of a barren land, the kingdom of Eldoria in ruins around him. The sky was dark, the land scorched and lifeless, and he saw shadows moving through the ruins—remnants of people he once knew, their faces filled with despair. In the distance, he saw Isadora, her magic weakened, struggling to defend a group of townsfolk against dark forces. Cedric was there too, his armour battered, his sword broken, yet he fought on, his face weary but determined.

Roderic, wounded but still defiant, stumbled over to Finn, his face filled with both anger and desperation. "Where were you, Finn?" he demanded, his voice raw. "Where were you when Eldoria needed you?"

Finn's heart ached as he looked at the destruction around him. He had set out to save the kingdom, but here he stood, surrounded by the ashes of what he had once loved. This was the cost of his failure, the kingdom lost because he had not been strong enough, not wise enough, to fulfil his duty.

He felt the weight of choice pressing down on him, a choice that would mean either bearing the crown's curse or abandoning his mission, and he realized the depth of the sacrifice he would have to make if he were to succeed.

With a jolt, he returned to the clearing, gasping as the visions faded. The witch stood before him, watching him closely, her expression unreadable.

"What did you see?" she asked softly, though Finn could tell she already knew.

Finn took a shuddering breath, the weight of what he had seen still lingering. "I saw... the cost. The cost of wearing the crown, of choosing to bear its curse. I saw what would happen if I failed, the kingdom reduced to ashes. And I saw... myself, becoming a shadow, a part of the land, forgotten by everyone I care about."

The witch nodded, her gaze sombre. "Now you understand, Finn. The crown's magic is both a blessing and a curse, binding its bearer to the land, demanding everything, even your very soul. Knowing this, do you still choose to carry it, to bear the burden for the sake of Eldoria?"

Finn looked at his friends—Cedric, Isadora, and Roderic—each of whom had stood by him through every trial, every sacrifice. He thought of the people of Eldoria, of the kingdom that had given him purpose, the home he had sworn to protect. He knew the cost was high, but he also knew that he couldn't walk away, not when the kingdom needed him.

"Yes," he said, his voice steady. "I'm willing to bear it. If it means saving Eldoria, I'll take on the curse. I'll do whatever it takes."

The witch's eyes softened, a glint of respect and perhaps even sadness in her gaze. "Then you have passed the final test, Finn. Worthiness is not found in power, but in sacrifice. You have shown that you are willing to give everything for the good of your people. And for that, you are worthy of the crown."

She reached into her cloak and withdrew a small amulet, its center a gemstone that glowed faintly with an ancient light. She pressed it into Finn's hand. "This amulet will aid you when the time comes, binding you to the land in a way that eases the crown's burden. It is a gift of protection, a shield against the darkness that the crown's curse brings."

Finn looked down at the amulet, feeling the warmth of its magic seep into him, a small comfort against the enormity of the sacrifice he was preparing to make. "Thank you," he said, his voice filled with gratitude.

The witch nodded once, then turned to leave, her figure fading into the mist. But just before she disappeared, she looked back, her expression gentle.

"Remember, Finn," she said softly, "sacrifice is a choice, but so is hope. The land remembers those who serve it, and sometimes, even the greatest burdens can be shared."

With that, she vanished, leaving Finn and his friends alone in the clearing.

They stood in silence for a moment, each of them absorbing the weight of what had just transpired. Then, Isadora stepped forward, placing a hand on Finn's shoulder. "You're not alone in this, Finn. Whatever the cost, we'll be there beside you."

Cedric gave him a firm nod, his gaze filled with pride. "You've proven yourself worthy, Finn. And we'll see this through together."

Roderic managed a wry smile, his voice softer than usual. "I'm not exactly hero material, but I'll be here. Loyalty and all that."

With a renewed sense of purpose, Finn held the amulet close, feeling its warmth steady him. The witch's final test had shown him the true weight of his choice, but he knew that, with his friends by his side, he was ready to face it.

Together, they turned toward the path back to Eldoria, the crown now within reach, their mission clear. They would restore the kingdom, not just with magic, but with the strength of their loyalty, the power of their sacrifice, and the unwavering bond they shared.

Chapter 26: The Temple of Lost Kings

The journey to the Temple of Lost Kings took Finn and his companions deeper into the mountains, where the path grew rougher and the air colder. Mist clung to the rocks, and an ancient stillness filled the air, as though even the wind dared not disturb the place they were approaching. It was said that the Temple of Lost Kings was built by Eldoria's first rulers, hidden away to protect the crown and its secrets until it was needed again.

Finn could feel the crown's weight in his pack, its presence pulsing with a quiet energy, almost as if it sensed they were drawing near to the place where it had once rested. The blood moon still hung faintly in the early morning sky, casting a reddish glow over the rocky landscape, adding to the sense of foreboding that surrounded them.

Finally, they reached a clearing, and there, carved into the side of a towering mountain, was the temple. It was an imposing structure, hewn from dark stone and decorated with intricate carvings of Eldoria's history. Pillars lined the entrance, each one engraved with the faces of past kings, their eyes downcast, as though guarding secrets they dared not reveal.

Roderic let out a low whistle, his gaze fixed on the towering entrance. "Well, I can see why they call it the Temple of Lost Kings. Looks like everyone who's ever ruled this kingdom has a piece of themselves here."

Cedric nodded, his voice solemn. "This temple was more than just a resting place for the crown. It was built as a sanctuary—a place where the past kings could prepare themselves to bear the crown's curse."

Isadora studied the carvings on the pillars, her fingers tracing the stone. "Each king who wore the crown left a piece of themselves here, a memory, a lesson. They built this temple to ensure that whoever bore the crown would understand the weight of their choice."

Finn felt a shiver run down his spine as he looked at the solemn faces etched into the stone. He couldn't help but wonder if one day, his own face would be carved here, a silent guardian watching over those who would follow. He pushed the thought aside, focusing instead on the path ahead.

The team entered the temple, stepping into the cool shadows that seemed to swallow the morning light. Torches lined the walls, their flames faintly flickering as if they had been recently lit, casting long shadows across the stone floor. The air was thick with the scent of old earth and ancient magic, a quiet reminder that this place was sacred.

As they moved deeper into the temple, they entered a vast chamber, its walls lined with statues of past kings, each one holding a different weapon, their faces etched with a mixture of pride and sorrow. In the center of the room stood a raised platform, upon which lay an empty pedestal, clearly intended to hold the crown.

Finn approached the pedestal, his gaze drawn to the words inscribed along its edge. The inscription was written in the old language of Eldoria, but he could make out its meaning: "To bear the crown is to give oneself to the land. A king's heart is not his own, but belongs to his people."

Isadora read the inscription aloud, her voice reverent. "It's a reminder of the sacrifice that every king has made. The crown is not just a symbol of power—it's a bond, one that requires the bearer to surrender everything for the sake of the kingdom."

Finn took a deep breath, the weight of the crown seeming heavier with each step. He had known, ever since uncovering the curse, that the choice he was making was not without cost. But seeing this temple, the faces of those who had come before him, deepened his understanding of what it truly meant to bear the crown.

Cedric stepped forward, his face lined with both pride and sorrow. "This place was built so that each king would understand the true nature of their duty. It's a place of reckoning, a place where they could confront their fears and find the strength to bear the burden of the crown."

Roderic, uncharacteristically quiet, studied the statues, his gaze lingering on the solemn faces. "These kings... they chose this. They accepted it, knowing what it would take from them. They didn't turn away."

Finn looked at his friends, feeling a swell of gratitude for their support, for the journey they had taken together. "This is where I have to make my choice," he said quietly. "To take on the crown's curse, to bind myself to the kingdom, or... to leave it here, where it might be found by someone else in another time of need."

Isadora placed a gentle hand on his shoulder. "Whatever you choose, Finn, you won't face it alone. We're here with you, no matter what."

He nodded, drawing strength from her words. With a deep breath, he pulled the crown from his pack and unwrapped it, placing it carefully on the pedestal. The crown seemed to glow with a faint, ethereal light, as though responding to the temple's magic. Its jewels sparkled in the dim light, casting patterns of color across the walls.

Suddenly, the ground beneath them trembled, and a low rumble echoed through the chamber. The statues' eyes seemed to gleam, their expressions shifting from stoic to watchful, as though the temple itself were coming to life.

The witch's voice filled the room, echoing from somewhere unseen, her tone calm yet laced with warning. "You have reached the place of reckoning, Finn. Here, the spirits of the past kings will test you, to see if you are truly worthy to bear the crown."

From the shadows, ghostly figures began to materialize, each one a spectral king, their forms shrouded in mist. They surrounded the platform, their faces solemn and grave. Finn felt his heart pound, but he held his ground, meeting their gazes with quiet determination.

One of the kings, his face lined with wisdom and sorrow, stepped forward. His voice was deep and filled with the weight of centuries. "Why do you seek to bear the crown, knowing the curse it holds? Are you truly willing to surrender yourself for Eldoria, to give up your own life for the kingdom?"

Finn swallowed, his voice steady as he answered. "I seek to bear the crown because Eldoria needs a protector. I understand the cost, and I am willing to pay it, to give myself to the land if it means that the kingdom will be safe."

Another spirit, younger and fiercer, with eyes that burned with a quiet intensity, spoke next. "Many before you have tried to wield this power for glory, for ambition. How do you know that your heart is pure, that you will not be tempted to use the crown's magic for yourself?"

Finn took a deep breath, looking at his friends, who stood behind him, their faces filled with pride and loyalty. "I am not alone. My friends have been with me through every trial, every test. I am here for them, for the kingdom, and I know that they will keep me true to my purpose."

The spirits exchanged glances, murmuring among themselves, their voices blending into a low hum. Finally, the first spirit stepped forward once more, his gaze softening.

"You have shown courage and selflessness, Finn. But the crown's curse is powerful, and it will take much from you. Are you certain you are ready to give yourself to the land, to become a part of Eldoria in a way that few understand?"

Finn nodded, feeling a sense of calm settle over him. "I am ready. I accept the burden of the crown, not for myself, but for the people of Eldoria."

The spirits nodded in unison, and the room filled with a bright, ethereal light. The crown rose from the pedestal, hovering in the air, and then slowly descended, settling onto Finn's head. As it did, he felt a surge of power, a connection to the land itself—a bond that ran deep, intertwining his life with Eldoria's magic.

He could feel the presence of the past kings, their wisdom and strength flowing into him, guiding him, reassuring him. He knew that he was not alone, that he was part of something far greater than himself.

The spirits faded, their voices a final whisper in the air. "Bear the crown with honour, young squire, and may the strength of Eldoria be with you always."

As the light faded, Finn looked at his friends, feeling both humbled and empowered. They gathered around him, each of them placing a hand on his shoulder, grounding him, sharing the weight of his choice.

Isadora's eyes shone with pride and tears. "You did it, Finn. You've become more than a squire—you're Eldoria's protector now."

Cedric nodded, his gaze filled with respect. "You have earned your place among the legends, Finn. The kingdom could ask for no better guardian."

Roderic smirked, though his eyes held a hint of admiration. "Not bad, squire. Not bad at all."

With the crown's magic flowing through him, Finn felt a renewed sense of purpose. He knew that his life would now be forever tied to Eldoria, that he would slowly fade, as every king before him had. But he also knew that he was ready, that he had the strength to bear the crown's curse, to protect the kingdom he loved.

Together, they left the Temple of Lost Kings, stepping into the dawn light, their path clear, their mission fulfilled. Eldoria had its protector, a squire who had proven himself worthy of the crown, and as they journeyed back to the kingdom, they carried with them the knowledge that some sacrifices were worth every cost.

For Finn, for his friends, and for the kingdom, the story of the lost crown had reached its end—and a new chapter, one of hope and honour, had begun.

Chapter 27: A Race Against Shadows

The first rays of dawn painted the landscape in pale gold as Finn and his companions left the Temple of Lost Kings, the crown of Eldoria now resting upon Finn's head. The ancient magic within it pulsed in time with his heartbeat, connecting him to the land in a way that was both empowering and unsettling. He could feel Eldoria's energy coursing through him, but he could also sense the weight of the curse, a constant reminder of the sacrifice he had accepted.

They moved quickly, following the narrow mountain path that would take them back to the kingdom. But just as they reached the edge of the clearing, the shadows around them began to shift. An unnatural darkness crept over the land, smothering the dawn's light, and a chill filled the air. Finn's senses tingled with an unsettling awareness—something was watching them, something that didn't want the crown to leave the temple.

Isadora halted, her eyes wide. "Do you feel that? There's dark magic here... it's like the shadows themselves are alive."

Cedric drew his sword, his gaze sweeping over the darkening landscape. "Whatever it is, it's coming for us. We need to move."

From the edges of the clearing, shadowy figures began to materialize, their forms twisting and shifting as though they were made of darkness itself. Their eyes glowed with a faint, malevolent light, and their shapes were vaguely human but stretched, elongated, as if corrupted by something ancient and dark. They moved silently, gliding across the ground with eerie precision, blocking every path away from the temple.

Roderic swallowed, his usual bravado momentarily faltering. "I don't suppose these are the friendly kind of shadows?"

Finn shook his head, his pulse quickening. He could feel the crown's magic respond to the presence of these creatures, pulsing with a warning, as though it, too, sensed the danger. "These shadows... they're part of the temple's curse. Guardians, meant to keep the crown hidden from anyone who tries to leave with it."

The shadow creatures began to advance, their movements slow but deliberate, as if savouring the hunt. Finn raised a hand, channelling the crown's energy, and a faint glow surrounded him, casting a shield around his friends.

"We have to move!" he said urgently, glancing back at the narrow mountain path that would take them down the cliffside. "These creatures won't stop until the crown is hidden again. They're part of the temple's magic, bound to keep its secrets."

With the shield protecting them for the moment, they bolted toward the path, running down the steep, rocky trail as fast as they dared. The shadow creatures followed, gliding over the ground with unnatural speed, closing the distance with every second. Finn could feel the weight of the crown pressing down on him, both a source of strength and a burden, its magic amplifying his awareness of the shadows' intentions.

"They're gaining on us!" Isadora called, her voice filled with fear as she glanced back.

Finn gritted his teeth, focusing on the crown's power. He extended his hand, sending a wave of light down the path. The light flared, momentarily halting the shadows, but the creatures merely reformed, their shapes shifting and solidifying once more as they resumed the pursuit.

"They're relentless," Cedric said, swinging his sword at a shadow creature that had darted too close. His blade passed through it, the darkness dissipating only to reform seconds later. "Our weapons won't hold them off."

Isadora's eyes flashed with determination. "They're made of magic. Let me try something."

She raised her hands, muttering an incantation under her breath. A sphere of radiant energy appeared between her palms, and with a shout, she hurled it at the nearest shadow creature. The light collided with the darkness, dissolving it with a sizzle. The creature let out a shriek, then vanished, its form dispersing like mist.

"It worked!" she cried, her face brightening. "But I don't have the strength to keep that up for long."

The shadows continued to close in, more of them emerging from the rocky terrain, their numbers seemingly endless. It was clear that the temple had released its entire arsenal of guardians, determined to retrieve the crown no matter the cost.

Roderic, breathing heavily, scanned the path ahead. "We can't keep running forever. If there's another way, now's the time to try it."

Finn felt the crown pulse again, its magic urging him to tap into its deeper reserves. He could sense a hidden well of power, an ancient magic that had protected Eldoria for centuries. But he also knew that using the crown's magic would come at a cost, accelerating the curse's grip on him. Yet in that moment, he realized he had no choice.

"Keep going!" he shouted to his friends, slowing his pace. "I'll hold them off."

Isadora turned, her face stricken. "Finn, no! You don't have to do this alone."

He gave her a reassuring look, his resolve unshaken. "This is what the crown demands, what it means to protect Eldoria. I'll catch up—I promise."

With a final nod, he turned to face the shadows, raising his hand as the crown's power surged through him. Light burst from his fingertips, enveloping the path and creating a barrier of shimmering energy that blocked the shadow creatures from advancing. The creatures shrieked, recoiling from the light, but they began to claw at the barrier, determined to break through.

The barrier wouldn't hold for long; Finn could feel the drain on his strength, the crown's magic pulling at his life force, binding him to the land even as he wielded it.

His friends paused just a few steps ahead, looking back at him with expressions of worry and admiration. Cedric, his face lined with pride, gave a small nod. "We'll be waiting for you, Finn. Don't keep us waiting too long."

With that, they continued down the path, leaving Finn to face the shadows alone. He gritted his teeth, focusing all his energy on maintaining the barrier. But he knew that as soon as he released it, the creatures would surge forward again.

He glanced up at the sky, where the blood moon still cast its ominous light, strengthening the curse and fuelling the temple's dark magic. He knew he couldn't defeat these creatures on his own, but he could at least buy his friends enough time to escape.

With a deep breath, he called upon the crown's magic once more, reaching into its ancient reserves. A powerful wave of light exploded from him, flooding the mountainside with brilliance, dissolving the shadows closest to him and sending the others scattering back. For a brief moment, he felt the immense, ancient power of the crown coursing through him, a bond between himself and the land that transcended time.

But the cost was immediate. Finn felt his strength wane, his vision blurring, as though a piece of his soul had been pulled into the earth itself, tying him even more closely to Eldoria. He staggered, his legs nearly giving out, but he forced himself to move, to follow the path where his friends had gone.

When he reached them, they helped him up, each of them lending their strength to support him. Finn looked at their faces, filled with concern, loyalty, and pride. The shadows had fallen back for now, but he knew that the curse's guardians would continue to pursue them, drawn to the crown as long as he held it.

"Thank you," Finn whispered, his voice weak but filled with gratitude.

Isadora squeezed his shoulder. "You don't have to thank us. We're in this together, remember?"

Cedric nodded, his gaze filled with respect. "You've shown us what it truly means to be worthy of the crown, Finn. Whatever comes next, we'll face it together."

With his friends by his side, Finn felt a renewed strength, his resolve bolstered by their loyalty. Together, they left the mountains, putting as much distance as they could between themselves and the temple. The blood moon's influence waned as the dawn finally broke, its crimson light fading, leaving the land bathed in soft, golden sunlight.

They had escaped the shadows, but Finn knew that the crown's curse would continue to test him, to demand more with each passing day. And yet, with his friends beside him, he felt ready to bear that burden, knowing that their loyalty and love would be his strength.

As they reached the outskirts of Eldoria, he looked back one last time, the Temple of Lost Kings barely visible in the distance. He knew that the shadows would always be a part of him now, a reminder of the sacrifice he had chosen. But he also knew that he had not faced them alone.

With a final, steady breath, he turned toward the kingdom, ready to fulfil his duty and protect Eldoria, no matter the cost. The race against shadows was over, but his journey as the kingdom's protector had only just begun.

Chapter 28: The Fall of the Betrayer

The journey back to Eldoria was filled with an uneasy silence. Though Finn and his companions had escaped the shadow creatures that guarded the Temple of Lost Kings, he couldn't shake a lingering feeling of dread. The crown's weight was heavier than ever, its curse pulling at his strength, but it was more than that—he sensed something darker at work, a tension that seemed to press in from all sides.

As they reached the outskirts of Eldoria, the mood grew tense. The moon had faded, but an unnatural stillness filled the air, as though the kingdom itself were holding its breath. Finn's gaze swept over his companions, each of whom bore signs of exhaustion, their faces lined with worry and determination.

Just as they approached the gates, Roderic stopped, his expression unreadable as he looked at Finn, then back at the crown. His eyes held a glint of something that Finn hadn't noticed before—a mix of envy, frustration, and regret. Finn felt a prickle of unease as he met Roderic's gaze, his instincts warning him that something was wrong.

"Roderic?" Finn asked, his voice cautious. "Is something on your mind?"

Roderic's face twisted into a bitter smile. "Oh, I have a lot on my mind, actually. More than I ever let on."

Finn glanced at Isadora and Cedric, who looked equally concerned. "What are you talking about?" Finn asked, keeping his voice steady.

Roderic took a step back, his hand drifting to the hilt of his dagger. "Do you know what it's like, Finn? To be nothing but a shadow, always watching someone else take the glory? I've watched you go from a simple squire to the one chosen to bear the crown, to be Eldoria's hero. But what about me? What have I gained from this journey?"

Cedric's face hardened, understanding dawning on him. "You're saying that all this time... you've been waiting for a chance to betray us?"

Roderic's expression grew colder, and he nodded slowly. "Betrayal is such a strong word, Cedric. Let's just say... I've been keeping my options open. I didn't come on this quest for loyalty or honour. I came for one thing: power. And now that the crown is within reach, I'm not about to let it slip through my fingers."

Isadora's eyes widened with anger and disbelief. "You would betray us, after everything we've been through together? You would turn your back on your friends, on the kingdom?"

Roderic laughed, though there was no warmth in it. "Friends? You're all so noble, so convinced that you're doing this for the greater good. But you don't understand what it's like to live in the shadows, to constantly be overlooked. I deserve a place in Eldoria's history, and if that means taking the crown for myself, then so be it."

Finn took a steadying breath, feeling both hurt and anger rise within him. "Roderic, the crown is a curse. It's not a path to power—it's a sacrifice. Do you even understand what you're trying to take?"

Roderic's eyes glinted with a fierce desperation. "Sacrifice or not, it's better than being nothing. With the crown, I'll finally have what I've always wanted—control, influence, a place in the kingdom that no one can take away."

He drew his dagger, his stance ready, and Finn realized with a sinking heart that there would be no talking him out of this. Roderic had made his choice, and it was clear he would stop at nothing to claim the crown for himself.

Cedric stepped forward, but Finn held up a hand, signalling for him and Isadora to stay back. "This is between me and Roderic," he said, his voice steady. "It's my responsibility."

Roderic smirked, his dagger glinting in the light. "Think you're up for this, Finn? You might be the kingdom's chosen protector, but I'm not going to make it easy for you."

Finn drew his sword, his gaze unwavering. "I don't want to fight you, Roderic. But I won't let you take the crown. Not after everything we've been through."

Roderic lunged forward, his movements quick and precise. Finn blocked the attack, their weapons clashing with a sharp ring that echoed through the air. Roderic was fast, his strikes calculated, each one aimed to disarm or injure. But Finn's training, honed through the trials of their journey, gave him the strength to hold his ground.

The duel was fierce, each blow a reflection of their clashing ideals. Roderic fought with desperation, each strike filled with years of resentment and frustration. But Finn fought with purpose, his resolve unbreakable, each movement driven by his commitment to protect the kingdom and his friends.

As they fought, Finn's mind raced with memories of their journey together—the battles they had faced, the dangers they had overcome, and the trust he had placed in Roderic. It pained him to see his friend consumed by ambition, but he knew that he couldn't let Roderic's betrayal endanger the kingdom.

Roderic's face twisted with anger as he launched another attack, his dagger flashing toward Finn's heart. But Finn anticipated the move, sidestepping and deflecting the blow, his sword grazing Roderic's arm. Roderic stumbled back, clutching his wounded arm, his expression a mix of shock and fury.

"You... you think you're better than me," Roderic spat, his voice filled with bitterness. "You think you deserve the crown more than I do."

Finn met his gaze, his voice calm but filled with conviction. "It's not about who deserves the crown, Roderic. It's about who is willing to bear its curse, to make the sacrifice. You want power, but that's not what the crown offers. It's a burden, a responsibility, and it's one that I chose willingly to protect Eldoria."

Roderic sneered, his grip on his dagger tightening. "You're a fool, Finn. You're throwing away your life for a kingdom that will forget you the moment you're gone."

Finn shook his head, his gaze steady. "If that's the cost of protecting Eldoria, then I'm willing to pay it."

With a final surge of determination, Roderic lunged, his desperation driving him forward. But Finn was ready. He sidestepped and twisted, using Roderic's momentum against him, disarming him with a swift, controlled movement. Roderic's dagger clattered to the ground, and he stumbled, falling to his knees.

Finn pointed his sword at Roderic, his heart heavy with both relief and sorrow. "It's over, Roderic. This doesn't have to end in violence. Surrender, and we'll find a way to set things right."

But Roderic's face twisted with anger and despair. "You think you've won, but you'll regret this, Finn. The crown will consume you, just as it consumed every king before you. You're nothing more than a sacrifice."

Finn lowered his sword, the sadness in his eyes undeniable. "Perhaps. But it's my choice. And I won't let your ambition destroy everything we've fought to protect."

Isadora and Cedric stepped forward, their expressions filled with both relief and sadness. Cedric placed a hand on Roderic's shoulder, his voice gentle but firm. "You had a choice, Roderic. You could have stood with us, but you chose this path. Let's end it here, before any more damage is done."

For a moment, Roderic's expression softened, a flicker of regret in his eyes. But then he looked away, his jaw clenched, refusing to meet their gaze. Cedric and Isadora exchanged a sombre look, and together, they led him away, ensuring he would no longer be a threat.

As the dawn broke over Eldoria, casting the kingdom in a warm, golden light, Finn felt the weight of his choice settle over him, even heavier than the crown itself. The battle had been won, but the price of Roderic's betrayal lingered, a reminder of the cost that ambition and jealousy could exact.

Isadora stepped beside him, her hand resting gently on his shoulder. "You did what you had to, Finn. Roderic made his choice, but you stayed true to who you are."

Finn nodded, his gaze fixed on the horizon. "It's just... I never wanted it to end like this. We were supposed to protect Eldoria together."

Cedric joined them, his voice filled with quiet pride. "You've proven yourself worthy, Finn. Not just of the crown, but of the loyalty of your friends and the trust of your kingdom. We're here, and we're with you. Eldoria is safe because of your courage."

With a final, steadying breath, Finn looked out over the kingdom he had sworn to protect, the kingdom he would now carry within himself as its guardian. The fall of the betrayer had been a painful chapter in their journey, but it had strengthened his resolve, a reminder of the true cost of power and loyalty.

As he turned to face his friends, he felt a renewed sense of purpose. Together, they would protect Eldoria, not for glory or ambition, but for the love and loyalty that had brought them this far.

And with the rising sun casting its light over the kingdom, Finn knew that, no matter the challenges that lay ahead, they would face them as a united force—loyal to each other, loyal to Eldoria. The crown's curse was his to bear, but he would carry it not as a burden, but as a mark of honour, a legacy forged through sacrifice and resilience.

Act 5: The Dawn of Hope

Chapter 29: The Last Stand at the Castle Gates

As Finn and his companions approached the gates of Eldoria, they were met with a sight that chilled them to the bone. The castle, once a beacon of strength and unity, was now surrounded by dark, twisted forces. Shadows stretched across the courtyard, and flickering flames illuminated a host of figures gathered at the gates. These were not mere soldiers—they were cloaked in dark magic, their eyes glowing with a sinister light, each one bearing the mark of those who had cursed the crown centuries ago.

Finn's heart pounded as he took in the scene. These were the remnants of the ancient cult—the Order of the Dark Veil—who had first cursed the crown to bind it with the kingdom's magic. They were the original guardians of the curse, intent on keeping Eldoria's rulers in eternal servitude to the land, siphoning the life force of each king to fuel their dark powers.

"They've come to reclaim the crown," Isadora whispered, her voice filled with dread. "If they seize it, they'll plunge the kingdom into darkness and use its power for their own ends."

Cedric's face was grim as he unsheathed his sword. "Then we make our stand here. For Eldoria."

Finn nodded, feeling the crown's weight settle on his head like a final acceptance of his role. The power of the crown pulsed within him, connecting him to the kingdom's magic, and he could feel it urging him to protect Eldoria, to rise against the darkness that threatened it. The curse he had taken on demanded a sacrifice, yes—but it also granted him the strength to protect his people, to face the very forces that had bound the crown in darkness.

"We end this here and now," Finn said, his voice strong and resolute. "For Eldoria. For the people. They will not take this kingdom."

With his friends by his side, Finn led the charge toward the castle gates, where the cultists were chanting in an ancient, guttural language, their voices merging into a dark symphony that sent shivers down his spine. They raised their hands, summoning shadows that twisted and writhed, forming barriers of dark energy. But Finn held the crown's power close, his determination unwavering.

The first wave of cultists charged forward, their weapons gleaming with an unholy light. Finn raised his sword, channelling the crown's magic through it, and a brilliant beam of energy shot forward, striking the cultists with a blinding light. They cried out, recoiling as the light burned through their dark shields, their forms disintegrating into shadows that dissipated in the air.

But for every cultist that fell, two more took their place, each one driven by a fanatical loyalty to the curse and the power it promised. They closed in, chanting louder, their hands reaching out with fingers that seemed to stretch like claws, grasping for the crown, for the ancient power that lay within it.

Isadora summoned a protective barrier of light, shielding them from the dark spells that crackled in the air like bolts of black lightning. "Finn, they're after you! The crown's power is calling to them!"

Roderic, wielding his twin daggers with speed and precision, struck down a cultist who had managed to slip past Cedric. He glanced at Finn, his face filled with both determination and urgency. "We can't hold them off forever! There has to be a way to break their connection to the crown."

Finn's mind raced, his thoughts turning to the magic bound within the crown. If the curse was linked to the land, perhaps there was a way to sever that link, to weaken the cultists' hold over it. But he knew it would come at a price—he would have to surrender a part of himself to strengthen the crown's magic, to create a protective barrier that would sever the cultists' connection.

"Keep them back!" he shouted, focusing all his energy on the crown. "I'm going to end this!"

Cedric and Roderic positioned themselves in front of him, their weapons ready as they formed a defensive line, fending off the cultists who surged forward with renewed fury. Isadora continued to cast spells, weaving a protective web of light that held the dark forces at bay, but she was weakening, and Finn knew he had to act fast.

Closing his eyes, he summoned the crown's magic, feeling it course through him, filling him with the combined strength of every king who had ever worn it. The weight of their sacrifice, their pain, and their love for Eldoria surged through him, a reminder of the responsibility he had taken on.

He raised his hand, and a golden light radiated from the crown, illuminating the night like a second dawn. The cultists screamed, recoiling from the light, but Finn pushed forward, directing the magic outward, expanding it into a powerful barrier that surrounded the castle gates, cutting off the cultists from the crown's influence.

The barrier pulsed, bright and unyielding, and Finn could feel the strain on his body, the curse pulling at his very soul, demanding his strength, his essence. But he held firm, gritting his teeth as he poured everything he had into the barrier, creating a wall of light that repelled the cultists' dark magic.

The cultists hissed and shrieked, their forms flickering as the barrier severed their connection to the crown. One by one, they began to retreat, their shadows shrinking and dissipating in the light until they were little more than fading remnants of darkness. The leader of the cultists, a tall figure cloaked in black with a face as pale as death, snarled in fury, his eyes locked on Finn.

"You think you can defy us, boy?" the leader spat, his voice dripping with malice. "The crown's curse is eternal. You may repel us now, but the curse will consume you in the end."

Finn met the leader's gaze, his voice steady despite the toll the barrier was taking on him. "I will bear that curse if it means saving Eldoria. Your darkness has no place here."

With one final burst of light, the barrier expanded, forcing the leader and his remaining followers back into the shadows. Their forms wavered, weakened by the crown's magic, and with a final, furious cry, they dissolved into nothing, their hold on the castle broken.

The light around Finn flickered and dimmed as he collapsed to his knees, his energy nearly spent. The barrier faded, but the castle was safe—the cultists had been vanquished, their connection to the crown severed. Cedric and Isadora rushed to his side, helping him to his feet as he struggled to catch his breath.

"You did it, Finn," Cedric said, his voice filled with pride. "You broke their hold. The kingdom is safe."

Finn nodded, though he could feel the toll of the battle deep within him, the curse's pull stronger than ever. He knew that he was now bound to Eldoria in a way that could never be undone, that his life would be spent protecting the kingdom, his strength forever entwined with the land.

Isadora placed a gentle hand on his shoulder, her face both proud and sorrowful. "You've shown them what true strength looks like, Finn. The crown may be a curse, but you've transformed it into something far greater. You are Eldoria's guardian."

Roderic, his usual smirk softened, nodded with respect. "You've earned every bit of that crown, squire. I may not have believed in all this honour and loyalty stuff before, but... you changed that."

Finn managed a weary smile, looking at his friends, his heart filled with gratitude. They had faced darkness, betrayal, and unimaginable sacrifice, but they had emerged victorious, their loyalty and love for each other unbreakable.

With the first light of dawn illuminating the castle, Finn stood at the gates, the weight of the crown resting upon his head, its magic a quiet, steady presence within him. He had taken on the curse willingly, knowing that it would forever bind him to the land, that his life would be slowly claimed by the magic that protected Eldoria.

But he knew, with his friends by his side and the people of the kingdom standing behind him, that he could bear that weight. The Last Stand at the Castle Gates had proven one thing above all: the power of sacrifice, loyalty, and courage in the face of darkness.

Together, they walked through the gates, back into the heart of Eldoria, knowing that their journey was not over, but that they would face whatever came next with the same strength that had carried them this far.

Eldoria was safe, for now. And as its new guardian, Finn would ensure that it remained so, no matter what challenges lay ahead.

Chapter 30: Return of the King's Crown

The dawn was breaking over Eldoria as Finn, exhausted and bruised from the battle at the castle gates, made his way through the throne room. Cedric, Isadora, and Roderic walked silently beside him, each bearing their own wounds from the night's struggle but holding themselves with pride and resolve. They had come through the darkness together, and now, at long last, it was time to complete their mission.

At the center of the throne room lay the king, resting on a simple, draped platform. His face was pale, his breathing shallow. Though he had been unconscious for days, his presence still commanded respect, his dignity intact even in his vulnerable state. The curse, bound to the land through the crown, had drained his life and strength, leaving him in this fragile state, hovering between life and death.

Finn felt the crown's weight on his head, its ancient magic thrumming with a quiet but relentless pull. He had borne it for only a short time, yet he could feel the life-draining curse within it, a reminder of the sacrifice each king before him had made to keep Eldoria safe. His choice to carry the crown had been a temporary measure, a bridge until he could return it to its rightful place. Now, standing before the king, he knew it was time.

With reverence, he removed the crown from his head, feeling the release of its weight and the relief that came with it. Yet, there was a pang of sadness in his heart, a strange attachment that had grown between himself and the crown. For a brief time, he had felt connected to Eldoria's history, to the line of kings who had borne the crown's curse before him. Now, he would return it to the one who truly belonged to that legacy.

He took a steadying breath and looked back at his friends. Isadora gave him a small nod, her eyes filled with pride and encouragement. Cedric, his face lined with respect, held Finn's gaze, as if giving him silent strength. Roderic, standing a step behind, managed a faint smile that hinted at the loyalty he'd found in his heart despite his own doubts and struggles.

Turning back to the king, Finn stepped forward, cradling the crown carefully in his hands. The first rays of dawn crept through the tall windows of the throne room, casting a soft, golden light over the scene. He knelt beside the king, whispering words he had heard echoed throughout their journey, words that had taken on a new, deeper meaning.

"For Eldoria," he murmured, "for the people, and for the sacrifices made by those who came before."

With one last look at the king's peaceful face, Finn gently placed the crown upon his head. The instant the crown settled, a faint, shimmering light enveloped the king, almost like a glow of dawn itself, illuminating his features. Finn felt a powerful surge of energy rush through the room—a quiet but intense release of magic, as though the kingdom itself were exhaling, freed from the grip of the curse.

The curse was broken.

Yet, as they waited, the king remained still, his chest rising and falling in shallow breaths, his eyes closed, untouched by the dawn's light. Finn's heart sank slightly, the hope of seeing the king's gaze again now slipping into uncertainty.

Cedric stepped forward, his face filled with understanding and gentle reassurance. "The curse may have been lifted, but the king has been under its weight for a long time. It may take time for his spirit to return fully, for him to recover."

Isadora placed a comforting hand on Finn's shoulder. "He's free now, Finn. Thanks to you. You've done everything you could—more than anyone could have asked. His strength will return with time."

Finn nodded, feeling a mixture of relief and sadness. He knew he had fulfilled his duty, that the kingdom was no longer in the clutches of the curse. But a part of him had hoped to see the king awaken, to witness the moment when Eldoria's true ruler returned to his people.

Roderic cleared his throat, his usual sarcasm softened. "Well, if I may say so... not a bad job, squire. You saved the kingdom and, might I add, proved that loyalty is something real, something worth fighting for. You're a true knight, whether or not they give you the title."

A small smile broke across Finn's face, gratitude and exhaustion mingling within him. "Thank you, Roderic. And thank all of you. I couldn't have done this without you."

Cedric clapped a hand on his shoulder. "No, Finn. You showed us what it means to be willing to sacrifice everything for what's right. The kingdom is lucky to have someone like you in its service."

The morning light grew stronger, casting a warm glow over the throne room, a quiet reminder that a new day had begun for Eldoria. The curse had been lifted, the darkness pushed back, and the kingdom was safe once more.

A gentle murmur echoed through the throne room as attendants, guards, and nobles began to enter, drawn by the strange light that had filled the castle. They looked on in awe as they saw the king, his face peaceful beneath the crown, his expression freed from the pain and suffering he had borne so long.

One by one, they knelt, their respect for both the king and for the young squire who had restored the kingdom's hope clear in their eyes. Finn felt a deep, quiet pride, a sense of belonging and purpose that would stay with him for the rest of his life.

He looked at his friends, each of whom had fought alongside him, sacrificed, and endured for the same cause. They had all changed, each of them bound to this journey and to each other in ways that words could scarcely express.

As the dawn brightened, Finn turned back to the king, feeling a gentle sense of peace settle over him. The crown had been returned, the curse broken, and though the king had yet to awaken, he knew that Eldoria would be safe.

For now, and for whatever trials might come, they had succeeded.

And as they stood together, their gazes lifting to meet the dawn's first rays, they knew that their story—the story of the lost crown and the sacrifice it demanded—would be remembered as a tale of courage, loyalty, and hope for generations to come.

Chapter 31: The Squire's Reward

Days passed after the return of the crown, and the kingdom began to heal. Eldoria's people, hearing of the curse's breaking and the king's peaceful rest, felt a renewed sense of hope. Word spread quickly of the young squire who had braved unimaginable trials, facing both dark magic and betrayal, to restore peace to the land. But while the kingdom rejoiced, Finn and his companions waited, watching over the king with quiet vigilance, hoping for the moment he would finally awaken.

Then, one early morning, just as the light began to filter through the castle windows, a stir came from the throne room where the king lay. Finn, seated nearby, looked up, his heart pounding as he saw the king's eyes slowly open, adjusting to the morning light. The air in the room grew still as everyone present held their breath, watching as Eldoria's ruler took his first full, unencumbered breath in weeks.

The king's gaze settled on Finn, and a faint smile crossed his face. Though he was still weak, there was a warmth and clarity in his eyes that had been absent for so long. "Finn," he murmured, his voice soft but filled with gratitude. "I have heard of your courage... I have felt it, even in my dreams."

Finn knelt at the king's side, bowing his head. "Your Majesty, I only did what was needed to save Eldoria. The crown, the curse... I was honoured to bear it, even for a short time."

The king's smile grew, and he looked at Finn with a mixture of pride and affection. "Not many would have taken on such a burden so willingly, let alone a young squire. You have done more than restore the kingdom's hope; you have shown us the true meaning of loyalty and sacrifice. For that, I owe you a debt beyond measure."

At that, Cedric, Isadora, and Roderic stepped forward, their expressions filled with respect for both the king and for Finn. Cedric bowed his head. "Your Majesty, Finn proved himself every step of the way. He fought not only to save you but to protect us, to protect Eldoria. He is more than a squire—he is a leader."

Isadora nodded, her eyes shining with pride. "Without him, none of us would have made it. He has earned his place among those who protect Eldoria."

Roderic, always the rogue, managed a grin. "Not to sound too sentimental, Your Majesty, but I think even the shadows know better than to cross this 'squire' again."

The king chuckled softly, his gaze warm as he looked at each of them. "You are all loyal friends, and I see that your words ring true. Finn, rise and come forward."

Finn stood, his heart pounding, and stepped closer to the throne. The king took a deep breath, his voice growing stronger as he spoke.

"For your bravery, your loyalty, and your sacrifice, I would do more than honour you with words. Finn, you have proven yourself worthy of a place among Eldoria's most honoured knights, and it is time the kingdom recognizes your deeds."

With a nod to his attendants, the king was handed a ceremonial sword, its blade etched with the symbols of Eldoria's knights. The king raised it with a steady hand, his gaze meeting Finn's. "Kneel, Finn of Eldoria."

Finn knelt before the king, his heart filled with a mix of awe and humility. The king touched the sword to each of Finn's shoulders, his voice resonant as he spoke the ancient words of knighthood.

"By the power vested in me, and in gratitude for your service to Eldoria, I hereby bestow upon you the title of Knight of Eldoria. Rise, Sir Finn, protector of the kingdom."

A swell of pride filled Finn's heart as he rose, his gaze meeting the king's. He felt both the weight and honour of the title settle within him, a culmination of every sacrifice and every step he had taken along the journey. His friends beamed with pride, and a cheer rose from those who had gathered in the throne room, celebrating the kingdom's newest knight.

The king gestured for Finn to step closer, his voice lowering as he addressed him personally. "I would also offer you a place at my side, a position as one of Eldoria's honoured knights, to continue defending this kingdom as you see fit."

Finn bowed deeply, his voice steady. "Your Majesty, it would be my honour to serve."

The king placed a gentle hand on Finn's shoulder, his expression filled with a fatherly pride. "Eldoria will be safe with you among its guardians, Sir Finn. And know that, though the crown may be heavy, your courage has lifted its curse, giving this kingdom a chance at true peace."

In the days that followed, Eldoria celebrated not only the return of its king but also the valour of the squire-turned-knight who had saved them all. Finn's deeds were sung in ballads, his story told in every village and town across the kingdom. Children looked up to him with awe, and his fellow knights welcomed him as a brother in arms.

His friends remained by his side, each finding their own place within the kingdom. Cedric was named Captain of the Guard, his wisdom and strength respected by all. Isadora was honoured as a mage of the court, her knowledge of magic revered, her bond with the kingdom's magic deepened by their journey. And even Roderic, ever the rogue, was offered a position as a royal scout, trusted to protect Eldoria's borders with his cunning and loyalty.

One evening, as they gathered on the castle walls, looking out over the kingdom they had fought so hard to protect, Finn felt a quiet sense of peace settle over him. The crown, the curse, the journey—they were now part of his past, a foundation upon which he would build his future as a knight of Eldoria.

Roderic raised a flask, grinning. "To Sir Finn, the knight who made even shadows afraid to linger."

Cedric chuckled, his voice filled with pride. "To a true leader, whose courage brought us all through the darkest trials."

Isadora smiled, her eyes filled with warmth. "To a friend who showed us that loyalty and love are the greatest magic of all."

Finn smiled, lifting his own glass, his heart filled with gratitude and pride. "To all of you. For standing by me, for facing the darkness, and for believing in me when I needed it most. For Eldoria."

As they toasted to their journey and the bond they shared, the last light of day faded, casting the kingdom in a gentle twilight. Finn looked out over the land, feeling both humbled and grateful, knowing that he would forever be bound to Eldoria's future, its protector and its servant.

In his heart, he knew that the story of the lost crown and the curse had reached its end. But a new story, one of hope, honour, and friendship, had begun.

Sir Finn of Eldoria, once a humble squire, was now a knight, an honoured guardian of the kingdom he had fought to save. And with his friends by his side, he was ready to face whatever challenges lay ahead, knowing that the true strength of a knight came not from power, but from the courage to protect those he loved.

Chapter 32: A Kingdom Restored

The kingdom of Eldoria was alive with celebration. Banners flew from every tower, music filled the streets, and people gathered in joy and relief, their spirits lifted by the return of peace. Finn, now Sir Finn of Eldoria, found himself at the center of it all, a reluctant yet grateful hero. As the newly restored knight, he was showered with gratitude from villagers and nobles alike, each thanking him for the courage and loyalty that had saved them all.

The castle courtyard had been transformed for the festivities, decorated with flowers and lights that glowed like stars as evening fell. Tables were set with feasts, children ran about with wooden swords pretending to be brave knights, and the king himself presided over the festivities, his gaze filled with pride as he watched the kingdom celebrate.

Finn stood with his friends, each of them finding moments of joy in the festivities. Cedric's laughter was rare but genuine, Isadora shared stories of their journey with an audience of wide-eyed apprentices, and even Roderic was in good spirits, entertaining the crowd with tales of their adventure (with his own mischievous embellishments).

Yet despite the celebration around him, Finn felt a quiet restlessness growing within. The journey he had taken, the trials he had endured—it had changed him. He knew that, although the crown was safely back where it belonged and the kingdom was at peace, his purpose had only just begun.

As the evening wore on, the king called for Finn to join him on a small platform at the center of the courtyard. The crowd fell silent as Finn approached, and the king smiled, his eyes warm with both pride and respect.

"People of Eldoria," the king announced, his voice strong and filled with gratitude, "we gather here not only to celebrate the return of peace to our kingdom but to honour a young man whose courage and sacrifice have restored hope to us all. Sir Finn of Eldoria, step forward."

Finn took a steadying breath and stepped forward, bowing to the king. The crowd erupted into cheers, their voices echoing through the night, filling the air with their appreciation and respect.

The king raised a hand, calling for silence, and the crowd quieted once more. "Sir Finn has shown us what it means to be a true hero. He has not only saved my life and restored the crown but has also reminded us that strength lies not in power alone but in the willingness to protect those we love. Let his deeds be remembered for generations to come."

The crowd cheered again, and Finn couldn't help but feel a deep sense of pride and humility. Yet, as he looked out over the people, he felt that same restlessness, a whisper in his heart that there was more to discover, more to protect, more to learn about his kingdom and its hidden past.

After the ceremony, as the festivities resumed, Finn slipped away to a quiet balcony overlooking the kingdom. The night air was cool, filled with the scent of flowers and the sounds of laughter drifting up from below. He took a deep breath, letting the peace of the moment settle over him, though his thoughts remained on the journey ahead.

"You look like a man with something on his mind," a familiar voice said.

Finn turned to see Isadora standing beside him, her gaze thoughtful as she studied his expression. "Celebrating doesn't suit you, does it?" she asked, a knowing smile on her lips.

Finn chuckled, shaking his head. "It's not that I'm ungrateful. I'm honoured, truly. But… after everything we've been through, I can't help but wonder if there's more to the story. The crown's curse, the cultists who sought to claim it—it feels like there's so much we still don't understand."

Isadora nodded, her eyes distant as she looked out over the kingdom. "You're not wrong. There are whispers of other relics, ancient artifacts tied to Eldoria's history. The crown was only one piece of the legacy left by the founders of this kingdom. Who knows what else might be out there, hidden and waiting to be uncovered?"

Finn felt a thrill of excitement at her words, his restlessness shifting into determination. "If there are other relics, other secrets connected to the kingdom's past, then maybe it's our duty to find them. To ensure they don't fall into the wrong hands."

A voice from behind interrupted them. "Planning another adventure already, are we?"

Finn turned to see Cedric and Roderic joining them, both looking amused. Cedric's face held a trace of a smile, while Roderic's grin was wide and mischievous.

"You didn't think you'd go off on your own, did you?" Cedric asked, his tone both amused and resolute. "We've faced shadows, curses, and ancient magic together. Whatever lies ahead, we face it together."

Roderic clapped Finn on the back, winking. "Besides, who's going to tell the tales of our daring heroics if I'm not there to add a little flair to the story?"

Finn laughed, feeling a surge of gratitude for his friends. Each of them had faced incredible trials, yet here they stood, ready for whatever came next. They had become more than allies; they were family, bound not only by loyalty but by the experiences they had shared, the sacrifices they had made.

As they stood together on the balcony, watching the stars appear one by one in the night sky, Finn felt the weight of his new title, his duty, and his promise to the kingdom. But he no longer felt it as a burden. It was a calling, one that he was honoured to accept.

Isadora's voice was soft but filled with resolve. "There are ancient ruins in the south, near the borderlands. I've heard stories of an artifact connected to the same magic as the crown. If we leave by dawn, we could be there within a week."

Cedric nodded thoughtfully. "The borderlands are treacherous, but we've faced worse. And if there's a chance to protect Eldoria by recovering these relics, then it's worth the risk."

Roderic grinned, his eyes gleaming with excitement. "Sounds like another tale for the ages. And who knows? Maybe this time, I'll be the one to save everyone."

Finn looked at each of his friends, his heart filled with a fierce sense of purpose and anticipation. This journey, this calling—it was not just his, but theirs, a shared destiny to protect and uncover the hidden mysteries of Eldoria.

With a final glance over the kingdom, Finn raised his hand, as if sealing their promise to one another. "For Eldoria," he said, his voice steady.

The others joined him, their voices echoing his vow. "For Eldoria."

As the first light of dawn began to touch the horizon, Finn knew that a new adventure awaited them, one filled with unknown dangers, ancient secrets, and the unwavering bond of friendship. The kingdom had been restored, but the legacy of Eldoria stretched far beyond the crown, woven into the land, the people, and the relics that held its magic.

And as they left the castle, their eyes bright with the thrill of what lay ahead, Finn couldn't help but feel that this was only the beginning.

The squire had become a knight, the kingdom had gained its hero, and the legacy of Eldoria was waiting to be reclaimed, one relic at a time.

Disclaimer:

This book is a work of fiction. Names, characters, places, events, and incidents are products of the author's imagination or are used fictitiously. Any resemblance to actual persons, living or dead, or actual events is purely coincidental.

The depiction of magic, ancient relics, and curses are intended solely for fictional purposes and are not based on any real-world beliefs or practices. This story is set in a fantasy realm and is not intended to reflect or promote any specific ideologies or spiritual beliefs.

Readers should enjoy this book as a work of fantasy and entertainment. Any actions, views, or opinions expressed by characters are those of the characters alone and do not necessarily reflect the views of the author or publisher.

For readers of all ages, we hope you enjoy the adventure and embrace the magic of storytelling.

Milton Keynes UK
Ingram Content Group UK Ltd.
UKHW030912121124
451094UK00001B/102